GHOST CAMP

Look for other **Goosebumps** books
by R.L. Stine:

The Abominable Snowman of Pasadena
The Barking Ghost
The Cuckoo Clock of Doom
The Curse of the Mummy's Tomb
Deep Trouble
Egg Monsters From Mars
Ghost Beach
The Ghost Next Door
The Haunted Mask
The Horror at Camp Jellyjam
How I Got My Shrunken Head
How to Kill a Monster
It Came From Beneath the Sink!
Let's Get Invisible!
Monster Blood
Night of the Living Dummy
One Day at HorrorLand
Say Cheese and Die!
The Scarecrow Walks at Midnight
A Shocker on Shock Street
Stay Out of the Basement
Welcome to Camp Nightmare
Welcome to Dead House
The Werewolf of Fever Swamp

Goosebumps®

GHOST CAMP

R.L. STINE

SCHOLASTIC INC.
New York Toronto London Auckland Sydney
Mexico City New Delhi Hong Kong Buenos Aires

ISBN 0-439-56831-5

Copyright © 1996 by Scholastic Inc.

All rights reserved. Published by Scholastic Inc.
SCHOLASTIC, GOOSEBUMPS, and associated logos are trademarks and/or registered trademarks of Scholastic Inc.

12 11 10 9 8 7 6 5   6 7 8/0

Printed in the U.S.A.   40

First Scholastic printing, July 1996

1

"You know I get bus sick, Harry," Alex groaned.

"Alex, give me a break." I shoved my brother against the window. "We're almost there. Don't start thinking about getting bus sick now!"

The bus rumbled over the narrow road. I held onto the seat in front of me. I gazed out the window.

Nothing but pine trees. They whirred past in a blur of green. Sunlight bounced off the dusty glass of the window.

We're almost to Camp Spirit Moon, I thought happily.

I couldn't wait to get off the bus. My brother, Alex, and I were the only passengers. It was kind of creepy.

The driver was hidden in front of a green curtain. I had glimpsed him as Alex and I climbed on board. He had a nice smile, a great suntan, curly blond hair, and a silver earring in one ear.

"Welcome, dudes!" he greeted us.

Once the long bus ride began, we didn't see him or hear from him again. Creepy.

Luckily, Alex and I get along okay. He's a year younger than me. He's eleven. But he's as tall as I am. Some people call us the Altman twins, even though we're not twins.

We both have straight black hair, dark brown eyes, and serious faces. Our parents are always telling us to cheer up — even when we're in really good moods!

"I feel a little bus sick, Harry," Alex complained.

I turned away from the window. Alex suddenly looked very yellow. His chin trembled. A bad sign.

"Alex, pretend you're not on a bus," I told him. "Pretend you're in a car."

"But I get carsick, too," he groaned.

"Forget the car," I said. Bad idea. Alex can get carsick when Mom backs down the driveway!

It's really a bad-news habit of his. His face turns a sick yellow. He starts to shake. And then it gets kind of messy.

"You've got to hold on," I told him. "We'll be at camp soon. And then you'll be fine."

He swallowed hard.

The bus bounced over a deep hole in the road. Alex and I bounced with it.

"I really feel sick," Alex moaned.

"I know!" I cried. "Sing a song. That always

cures you. Sing a song, Alex. Sing it really loud. No one will hear. We're the only ones on the bus."

Alex loves to sing. He has a beautiful voice.

The music teacher at school says that Alex has perfect pitch. I'm not sure what that means. But I know it's a good thing.

Alex is serious about his singing. He's in the chorus at school. Dad says he's going to find a voice teacher for Alex this fall.

I stared at my brother as the bus bounced again. His face was about as yellow as a banana skin. Not a good sign.

"Go ahead — sing," I urged him.

Alex's chin trembled. He cleared his throat. Then he began to sing a Beatles song we both really like.

His voice bounced every time the bus bumped. But he started to look better as soon as he started to sing.

Pretty smart idea, Harry, I congratulated myself.

I watched the pine trees whir past in the sunlight and listened to Alex's song. He really does have an awesome voice.

Am I jealous?

Maybe a little.

But he can't hit a tennis ball the way I can. And I can beat him in a swim race every time. So it evens out.

3

Alex stopped singing. He shook his head unhappily. "I wish Mom and Dad signed me up for the music camp." He sighed.

"Alex, the summer is half over," I reminded him. "How many times do we have to go over this? Mom and Dad waited too long. It was too late."

"I know," Alex said, frowning. "But I wish — "

"Camp Spirit Moon was the only camp we could get into this late in the summer," I said. "Hey, look — !"

I spotted two deer outside the window, a tall one and a little baby one. They were just standing there, staring at the bus as it sped by.

"Yeah. Cool. Deer," Alex muttered. He rolled his eyes.

"Hey — lighten up," I told him. My brother is so moody. Sometimes I just want to shake him. "Camp Spirit Moon may be the coolest camp on earth," I said.

"Or it may be a dump," Alex replied. He picked at some stuffing that poked up from a hole in the bus seat.

"The music camp is so great." He sighed. "They put on *two* musicals each summer. That would have been so awesome!"

"Alex, forget about it," I told him. "Let's enjoy Camp Spirit Moon. We only have a few weeks."

The bus suddenly screeched to a stop.

Startled, I bounced forward, then back. I

turned to the window, expecting to see a camp out there. But all I could see were pine trees. And more pine trees.

"Camp Spirit Moon! Everybody out!" the driver called.

Everybody? It was just Alex and me!

The driver poked his blond head out from behind the curtain. He grinned at us. "How was the ride, dudes?" he asked.

"Great," I replied, stepping into the aisle. Alex didn't say anything.

The driver climbed out. We followed him around to the side of the bus. Bright sunlight made the tall grass sparkle all around us.

He leaned into a compartment and pulled out our bags and sleeping bags. He set everything down on the grass.

"Uh . . . where's the camp?" Alex asked.

I shielded my eyes with my hand and searched around. The narrow road curved through a forest of pine trees as far as I could see.

"Right through there, dudes," the driver said. He pointed to a dirt path that cut through the trees. "It's a real short walk. You can't miss it."

The driver shut the baggage compartment. He climbed back onto the bus. "Have a great time!" he called.

The door shut. The bus roared away.

Alex and I squinted through the bright sunlight at the dirt path. I swung my duffel bag over my shoulder. Then I tucked my sleeping bag under one arm.

"Shouldn't the camp send someone out here to greet us?" Alex asked.

I shrugged. "You heard the driver. He said it's a very short walk."

"But still," Alex argued. "Shouldn't they send a counselor to meet us out here on the road?"

"It's not the first day of camp," I reminded him. "It's the middle of the summer. Stop complaining about everything, Alex. Pick up your stuff, and let's get going. It's hot out here!"

Sometimes I just have to be the big brother and order him around. Otherwise, we won't get anywhere!

He picked up his stuff, and I led the way to the path. Our sneakers crunched over the dry red dirt as we made our way through the trees.

The driver hadn't lied. We'd walked only two or three minutes when we came to a small, grassy clearing. A wooden sign with red painted letters proclaimed CAMP SPIRIT MOON. An arrow pointed to the right.

"See? We're here!" I declared cheerfully.

We followed a short path up a low, sloping hill. Two brown rabbits scurried past, nearly in front of our feet. Red and yellow wildflowers swayed along the side of the hill.

When we reached the top, we could see the camp.

"It looks like a real camp!" I exclaimed.

I could see rows of little white cabins stretching in front of a round blue lake. Several canoes were tied to a wooden dock that stuck out into the lake.

A large stone building stood off to the side. Probably the mess hall or the meeting lodge. A round dirt area near the woods had benches around it. For campfires, I guessed.

"Hey, Harry — they have a baseball diamond *and* a soccer field," Alex said, pointing.

"Excellent!" I cried.

I saw a row of round red-and-white targets at the edge of the trees. "Wow! They have archery, too," I told Alex. I love archery. I'm pretty good at it.

I shifted the heavy duffel bag on my shoulder. We started down the hill to the camp.

We both stopped halfway down the hill. And stared at each other.

"Do you notice anything weird?" Alex asked.

I nodded. "Yeah. I do."

I noticed something *very* weird. Something that made my throat tighten and my stomach suddenly feel heavy with dread.

The camp was empty.

No one there.

2

"Where *is* everyone?" I asked, moving my eyes from cabin to cabin. No one in sight.

I squinted at the lake behind the cabins. Two small, dark birds glided low over the sparkling water. No one swimming there.

I turned to the woods that surrounded the camp. The afternoon sun had begun to lower itself over the pine trees. No sign of any campers in the woods.

"Maybe we're in the wrong place," Alex said softly.

"Huh? Wrong place?" I pointed to the sign. "How can we be in the wrong place? It says Camp Spirit Moon — doesn't it?"

"Maybe they all went on a field trip or something," Alex suggested.

I rolled my eyes. "Don't you know anything about camp?" I snapped. "You don't go on field trips. There's nowhere to go!"

"You don't have to *shout!*" Alex whined.

"Then stop saying such stupid things!" I replied angrily. "We're all alone in the woods in an empty camp. We've got to think clearly."

"Maybe they're all in that big stone building over there," Alex suggested. "Let's go check it out."

I didn't see any signs of life there. Nothing moved. The whole camp was as still as a photograph.

"Yeah. Come on," I told Alex. "We might as well check it out."

We were still about halfway down the hill, following the path through the tangles of pine trees — when a loud cry made us both stop and gasp in surprise.

"Yo! Hey! Wait up!"

A red-haired boy, in white tennis shorts and a white T-shirt, appeared beside us. I guessed he was sixteen or seventeen.

"Hey — where did you come from?" I cried. He really startled me. One second Alex and I were alone. The next second this red-haired guy was standing there, grinning at us.

He pointed to the woods. "I was gathering firewood," he explained. "I lost track of the time."

"Are you a counselor?" I asked.

He wiped sweat off his forehead with the front of his T-shirt. "Yes. My name is Chris. You're Harry and you're Alex — right?"

Alex and I nodded.

"I'm sorry I'm late," Chris apologized. "You weren't worried, were you?"

"Of course not," I replied quickly.

"Harry was a little scared. But I wasn't," Alex said. Sometimes Alex can really be a pain.

"Where is everyone?" I asked Chris. "We didn't see any campers, or counselors, or anyone."

"They all left," Chris replied. He shook his head sadly. When he turned back to Alex and me, I saw the frightened expression on his face.

"The three of us — we're all alone out here," he said in a trembling voice.

3

"Huh? They *left?*" Alex cried shrilly. "But — but — where did they go?"

"We *can't* be all alone!" I cried. "The woods — "

A smile spread over Chris's freckled face. Then he burst out laughing. "Sorry, guys. I can't keep a straight face." He put his arms around our shoulders and led us toward the camp. "I'm just joking."

"Excuse me? That was a joke?" I demanded. I was feeling very confused.

"It's a Camp Spirit Moon joke," Chris explained, still grinning. "We play it on all the new campers. Everyone hides in the woods when the new campers arrive at camp. Then a counselor tells them that the campers all ran away. That they're all alone."

"Ha-ha. Very funny joke," I said sarcastically.

"You always try to *scare* the new campers?" Alex asked.

Chris nodded. "Yeah. It's a Camp Spirit Moon

11

tradition. We have a lot of great traditions here. You'll see. Tonight at the campfire — "

He stopped when a big black-haired man — also dressed in white — came lumbering across the grass toward us. "Yo!" the man called in a booming, deep voice.

"This is Uncle Marv," Chris whispered. "He runs the camp."

"Yo!" Uncle Marv repeated as he stepped up to us. "Harry, what's up?" He slapped me a high five that nearly knocked me into the trees.

Uncle Marv grinned down at Alex and me. He was so *huge* — he reminded me of a big grizzly bear at the zoo back home.

He had long, greasy black hair that fell wildly over his face. Tiny, round blue eyes — like marbles — under bushy black eyebrows.

His arms bulged out from under his T-shirt. Powerful arms like a wrestler's. His neck was as wide as a tree trunk!

He reached down and shook Alex's hand. I heard a loud *crunch* and saw Alex gasp in pain.

"Good firm handshake, son," Uncle Marv told Alex. He turned to me. "Did Chris play our little 'Alone in the Woods' joke on you guys?" His voice boomed so loud, I wanted to cover my ears.

Does Uncle Marv ever whisper? I wondered.

"Yeah. He fooled us," I confessed. "I really thought there was no one here."

Uncle Marv's tiny blue eyes sparkled. "It's one

of our oldest traditions," he said, grinning. What a grin! It looked to me as if he had at least *six rows* of teeth!

"Before I take you to your cabin, I want to teach you the Camp Spirit Moon greeting," Uncle Marv said. "Chris and I will show it to you."

They stood facing each other.

"Yohhhhhhhh, Spirits!" Uncle Marv bellowed.

"Yohhhhhhhh, Spirits!" Chris boomed back.

Then they gave each other a left-handed salute, placing the hand on the nose, then swinging it straight out in the air.

"That's how Camp Spirit Moon campers greet each other," Uncle Marv told us. He pushed Alex and me together. "You two try it."

I don't know about you, but this kind of thing embarrasses me. I don't like funny greetings and salutes. It makes me feel like a jerk.

But I had just arrived at camp. And I didn't want Uncle Marv to think I was a bad sport. So I stood in front of my brother. "Yohhhhhhhh, Spirits!" I shouted. And I gave Alex a sharp nose salute.

"Yohhhhhhhh, Spirits!" Alex showed a lot more enthusiasm than I did. He likes this kind of thing. He flashed me a sharp salute.

Uncle Marv tossed back his head in a loud, bellowing laugh. "Very good, guys! I think you're both going to be great Camp Spirit Moon campers."

He winked at Chris. "Of course, the campfire tonight is the *real* test."

Chris nodded, grinning.

"The campfire tonight?" I asked. "A test?"

Uncle Marv patted my shoulder. "Don't worry about it, Harry."

Something about the way he said that made me worry a *lot*.

"All new campers come to a Welcoming Campfire," Chris explained. "It's a chance to learn our Camp Spirit Moon traditions."

"Don't tell them any more about it," Uncle Marv told Chris sharply. "We want them to be surprised — don't we?"

"Surprised — ?" I choked out.

Why did I suddenly have such a bad feeling? Why did my throat tighten up again? Why did I have a fluttering feeling in my chest?

"Do we sing camp songs at the Welcoming Campfire?" Alex asked. "I'm really into singing. I take voice lessons back home and — "

"Don't worry. You'll sing. Plenty," Uncle Marv interrupted in a low, almost menacing voice.

I caught the cold look in his tiny eyes — cold as blue ice. And I felt a shiver roll down my back.

He's trying to scare us, I thought. It's all a joke. He's having fun with us. He always tries to scare new campers. It's a Camp Spirit Moon tradition.

"I think you boys will enjoy the campfire tonight," Uncle Marv boomed. "If you survive it!"

He and Chris shared a laugh.

"Catch you later," Chris said. He gave Alex and me a nose salute and vanished into the woods.

"This will be your bunk," Uncle Marv announced. He pulled open the screen door of a tiny white cabin. "Whoa!" He nearly pulled the door off its hinges.

Alex and I dragged our duffels and sleeping bags into the cabin. I saw bunk beds against three of the walls. Narrow wooden chests of drawers. Cubbyholes for storing things.

The walls were white. A light dangling from the ceiling cast a bright glow. The afternoon sun sent orange rays through a small window above one of the bunk beds.

Not bad, I thought.

"That bunk is free," Uncle Marv told us, pointing to the bed against the window. "You can decide who gets the top and who gets the bottom."

"I need the bottom," Alex said quickly. "I toss and turn a lot at night."

"And he sings in his sleep," I told Uncle Marv. "Do you believe it? Alex is so into singing, he doesn't even stop when he's sleeping!"

"You will have to try out for the talent show," Uncle Marv told Alex. And then he repeated in a low voice, "If you survive tonight." He laughed.

Why did he keep saying that?

He's kidding, I reminded myself. Uncle Marv is just *kidding*.

"The boys' cabins are on the left," Uncle Marv told us. "And the girls' cabins are on the right. We all use the lodge and mess hall. It's that big stone building near the woods."

"Should we unpack now?" Alex asked.

Uncle Marv pushed back his greasy black hair. "Yes. Use any cubbies that are empty. You'd better hurry, guys. The rest of the campers will be back from the woods soon with firewood. It will be time for our campfire."

He gave us a "Yohhhhhhhh, Spirits!" and a sharp nose salute.

Then he turned and lumbered away. The screen door slammed hard behind him.

"Fun guy," I muttered.

"He's kind of scary," Alex admitted.

"He's just joking," I said. "All summer camps try to terrify the new campers. I think." I dragged my duffel bag over to the bed.

"But it's all in fun. There's nothing to be scared about, Alex," I told my brother. "Nothing at all."

I tossed my sleeping bag into the corner. Then I started toward the low dresser to see if I could find an empty drawer.

"Whoa — !" I cried out as my sneaker stuck on something.

I peered down.

A blue puddle.

My sneaker had landed in a sticky blue puddle.

"Hey — " I tugged my sneaker out. The blue

16

liquid was thick. It stuck to the bottom and sides of my shoe.

I glanced around the room.

And saw more blue puddles. A sticky blue puddle in front of every bed.

"What's going *on* here? What *is* this stuff?" I cried.

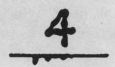

4

Alex had his bag open and was pulling stuff out and spreading it on the bottom bed. "What's your problem, Harry?" he called without turning around.

"It's some kind of blue slime," I replied. "Check it out. There are puddles all over the floor."

"Big deal," Alex muttered. He turned and glanced at the blue liquid stuck to my sneaker. "It's probably a camp tradition," he joked.

I didn't think it was funny. "Yuck!" I exclaimed. I reached down and poked my finger into the tiny, round puddle.

So cold!

The blue slime felt freezing cold.

Startled, I pulled my hand away. The cold swept up my arm. I shook my hand hard. Then I rubbed it, trying to warm it.

"Weird," I muttered.

Of course, everything got a lot weirder. In a hurry.

"Campfire time!"

Uncle Marv's cry through the screen door shook our cabin.

Alex and I spun to face the door. It had taken us forever to unpack our stuff. To my surprise, the sun had lowered. The sky outside the door was evening gray.

"Everyone is waiting," Uncle Marv announced. A gleeful smile spread over his face. His tiny eyes practically disappeared in the smile. "We all *love* the Welcoming Campfire."

Alex and I followed him outside. I took a deep breath. The air smelled fresh and piney.

"Wow!" Alex cried out.

The campfire was already blazing. Orange and yellow flames leaped up to the gray sky.

We followed Uncle Marv to the round clearing where the fire had been built. And saw the other campers and counselors for the first time.

They sat around the fire, all facing us. Watching us.

"They're all dressed alike!" I exclaimed.

"The camp uniform," Uncle Marv said. "I'll get you and Alex your camp uniforms tonight after the campfire."

As Alex and I neared the circle, the campers and counselors rose to their feet. A deafening "YOHHHHHHHHHH, SPIRITS!" shook the trees. Then a hundred left-handed nose salutes greeted us.

Alex and I returned the greeting.

Chris, the red-haired counselor, appeared beside us. "Welcome, guys," he said. "We're going to roast hot dogs on the fire before the campfire activities begin. So grab a stick and a hot dog, and join in."

The other kids were lining up in front of a long food table. I saw a huge platter of raw hot dogs in the center of the table.

As I hurried to get in line, several kids said hi to me.

"You're in my cabin," a tall boy with curly blond hair said. "It's the best cabin!"

"Cabin number seven rules!" a girl shouted.

"This is an awesome camp," the kid in front of me turned to say. "You're going to have a great time, Harry."

They seemed to be really nice kids. Up ahead, a boy and a girl were having a playful shoving match, trying to knock each other out of line. Other kids began cheering them on.

The fire crackled behind me. The orange light from its flames danced over everyone's white shorts and shirts.

I felt a little weird, not being dressed in white.

I was wearing an olive-green T-shirt and faded denim cutoffs. I wondered if Alex felt weird, too.

I turned and searched for him in the line. He was behind me, talking excitedly to a short blond boy. I felt glad that Alex had found a friend so fast.

Two counselors handed out the hot dogs. I suddenly realized I was *starving*. Mom had packed sandwiches for Alex and me to eat on the bus. But we were too excited and nervous to eat them.

I took the hot dog and turned to the crackling fire. Several kids were already huddled around the fire, poking their hot dogs on long sticks into the flames.

Where do I get a stick? I asked myself, glancing around.

"The sticks are over there," a girl's voice called from behind me — as if she had read my mind.

I turned and saw a girl about my age, dressed in white, of course. She was very pretty, with dark eyes and shiny black hair, pulled back in a ponytail that fell down her back. Her skin was so pale, her dark eyes appeared to glow.

She smiled at me. "New kids never know where to find the sticks," she said. She led the way to a pile of sticks leaning against a tall pine tree. She picked up two of them and handed one to me.

"Your name is Harry, right?" she asked. She had a deep, husky voice for a girl. Like she was whispering all the time.

"Yeah. Harry Altman," I told her.

I suddenly felt very shy. I don't know why. I turned away from her and shoved the hot dog onto the end of the stick.

"My name is Lucy," she said, making her way to the circle of kids around the fire.

I followed her. The kids' faces were all flickering orange and yellow in the firelight. The aroma of roasting hot dogs made me feel even hungrier.

Four girls were huddled together, laughing about something. I saw a boy eating his roasted hot dog right off the stick.

"Gross," Lucy said, making a disgusted face. "Let's go over here."

She led me to the other side of the campfire. Something popped in the fire. It sounded like a firecracker exploding. We both jumped. Lucy laughed.

We sat down on the grass, raised the long sticks, and poked our hot dogs into the flames. The fire was roaring now. I could feel its heat on my face.

"I like mine really black," Lucy said. She turned her stick and pushed it deeper into the flames. "I just love that burnt taste. How about you?"

I opened my mouth to answer her — but my

22

hot dog fell off the stick. "Oh no!" I cried. I watched it fall into the sizzling, red-hot blanket of flames.

I turned to Lucy. And to my surprise — to my *horror* — she leaned forward.

Stuck her hand deep into the fire.

Grabbed my hot dog from the burning embers and lifted it out.

5

I jumped to my feet. "Your hand!" I shrieked.

Yellow flames leaped over her hand and up her arm.

She handed me the hot dog. "Here," she said calmly.

"But your hand!" I cried again, gaping in horror.

The flames slowly burned low on her skin. She glanced down at her hand. Confused. As if she didn't know why I was in such a panic.

"Oh! Hey — !" she finally cried. Her dark eyes grew wide. "Ow! That was hot!" she exclaimed.

She shook her hand hard. Shook it until the flames went out.

Then she laughed. "At least I rescued your poor hot dog. Hope you like yours burned!"

"But — but — but — " I sputtered. I stared at her hand and arm. The flames had spread all over her skin. But I couldn't see any burns. Not a mark.

"The buns are over there," she said. "You want some potato chips?"

I kept staring at her hand. "Should we find the nurse?" I asked.

She rubbed her arm and wrist. "No. I'm fine. Really." She wiggled her fingers. "See?"

"But the fire — "

"Come on, Harry." She pulled me back to the food table. "It's almost time for the campfire activities to start."

I ran into Alex at the food table. He was still hanging out with the short blond boy.

"I made a friend already," Alex told me. He had a mouthful of potato chips. "His name is Elvis. Do you believe it? Elvis McGraw. He's in our cabin."

"Cool," I muttered. I was still thinking about the flames rolling up and down Lucy's arm.

"This is a great camp," Alex declared. "Elvis and I are going to try out for the talent show *and* the musical."

"Cool," I repeated.

I grabbed a hot dog bun and tossed some potato chips on my plate. Then I searched for Lucy. I saw her talking to a group of girls by the fire.

"Yohhhhhhhh, Spirits!" a deep voice bellowed. No way anyone could mistake that cry. It had to be Uncle Marv.

"Places around the council fire, everyone!" he ordered. "Hurry — places, everyone!"

Holding plates and cans of soda, everyone scurried to form a circle around the fire. The girls all sat together and the boys all sat together. I guessed each cabin had its own place.

Uncle Marv led Alex and me to a spot in the middle.

"Yohhhhhhhh, Spirits!" he cried again, so loud the fire trembled!

Everyone repeated the cry and gave the salute.

"We'll begin by singing our camp song," Uncle Marv announced.

Everyone stood up. Uncle Marv started singing, and everyone joined in.

I tried to sing along. But of course I didn't know the words. Or the tune.

The song kept repeating the line, "We have the spirit — and the spirit has us."

I didn't really understand it. But I thought it was pretty cool.

It was a long song. It had a lot of verses. And it always came back to: "We have the spirit — and the spirit has us."

Alex was singing at the top of his lungs. What a show-off! He didn't know the words, either. But he was faking it. And singing as loud as he could.

Alex is so crazy about his beautiful singing voice and his perfect pitch. He has to show it off whenever he can.

I gazed past my brother. His new friend, Elvis,

had his head tossed back and his mouth wide open. He was singing at the top of his lungs, too.

I think Alex and Elvis were having some kind of contest. Seeing who could sing the leaves off the trees!

The only problem? Elvis was a *terrible* singer!

He had a high, whiny voice. And his notes were all coming out sour.

As my dad would say, "He couldn't carry a tune in a wheelbarrow!"

I wanted to cover my ears. But I was trying to sing along, too.

It wasn't easy with the two of them beside me. Alex sang so loud, I could see the veins in his neck pulsing. Elvis tried to drown him out with his sour, off-key wails.

My face felt hot.

At first, I thought it was the heat from the blazing campfire. But then I realized I was blushing.

I felt so embarrassed by Alex. Showing off like that on his first night at camp.

Uncle Marv wasn't watching. He had wandered over to the girls' side of the fire, singing as he walked.

I slipped back, away from the fire.

I felt too embarrassed to stay there. I'll sneak back into place as soon as the song is over, I decided.

I just couldn't sit there and watch my brother act like a total jerk.

The camp song continued. "We have the spirit — and the spirit has us," everyone sang.

Doesn't the song ever end? I wondered. I backed away, into the trees. It felt a lot cooler as soon as I moved away from the fire.

Even back here, I could hear Alex singing his heart out.

I've got to talk to him, I told myself. I've got to tell him it isn't cool to show off like that.

"Ohh!" I let out a sharp cry as I felt a tap on my shoulder.

Someone grabbed me from behind.

"Hey — !" I spun around to face the trees. Squinted into the darkness.

"Lucy! What are *you* doing back here?" I gasped.

"Help me, Harry," she pleaded in a whisper. "You've got to help me."

A chill ran down my back. "Lucy — what's wrong?" I whispered.

She opened her mouth to reply. But Uncle Marv's booming voice interrupted.

"Hey, you two!" the camp director shouted. "Harry! Lucy! No sneaking off into the woods!"

The campers all burst out laughing. I could feel my face turning hot again. I'm one of those kids who blushes very easily. I hate it — but what can I do?

Everyone stared at Lucy and me as we made our way back to the fire. Alex and Elvis were slapping high fives and laughing at us.

Uncle Marv kept his eyes on me as I trudged back. "I'm glad you make friends so easily, Harry," he boomed. And all the campers started laughing at Lucy and me again.

I felt so embarrassed, I wanted to shrivel up and disappear.

But I was also worried about Lucy.

Had she followed me to the woods? Why?

Why did she ask me to help her?

I sat down between Lucy and Elvis. "Lucy —
what's wrong?" I whispered.

She just shook her head. She didn't look at me.

"Now I'm going to tell the two ghost stories,"
Uncle Marv announced.

To my surprise, some kids gasped. Everyone
suddenly became silent.

The crackling of the fire seemed to get louder.
Behind the pop and crack of the darting flames, I
heard the steady whisper of wind through the pine
trees.

I felt a chill on the back of my neck.

Just a cool breeze, I told myself.

Why did everyone suddenly look so solemn? So
frightened?

"The two ghost stories of Camp Spirit Moon
have been told from generation to generation,"
Uncle Marv began. "They are tales that will be
told for all time, for as long as dark legends are
told."

Across the fire, I saw a couple of kids shiver.

Everyone stared into the fire. Their faces were
set. Grim. Frightened.

It's only a ghost story, I told myself. Why is
everyone acting so weird?

The campers must have heard these ghost stories already this summer. So why do they look so
terrified?

I snickered.

How can *anyone* be afraid of a silly camp ghost story?

I turned to Lucy. "What's up with these kids?" I asked.

She narrowed her dark eyes at me. "Aren't you afraid of ghosts?" she whispered.

"Ghosts?" I snickered again. "Alex and I don't believe in ghosts," I told her. "And ghost stories never scare us. Never!"

She leaned close to me. And whispered in my ear: "You might change your mind — after tonight."

7

The flames flickered, crackling up to the dark, starry sky. Uncle Marv leaned into the orange firelight. His tiny, round eyes sparkled.

The woods suddenly became quiet. Even the wind stopped whispering.

The air felt cold on my back. I scooted closer to the campfire. I saw others move closer, too. No one talked. All eyes were on Uncle Marv's smiling face.

Then, in a low voice, he told the first ghost story. . . .

A group of campers went into the woods for an overnight. They carried tents and sleeping bags. They walked single file along a narrow dirt path that twisted through the trees.

Their counselor's name was John. He led them deeper and deeper into the woods.

Dark clouds floated overhead. When the clouds covered the full moon, the darkness swept over the campers. They walked close together, trying to see the curving path.

Sometimes the clouds moved away, and the moonlight poured down on them. The trees glowed, silvery and cold, like ghosts standing in the forest.

They sang songs at first. But as they moved deeper into the woods, their voices became tiny and shrill, muffled by the trees.

They stopped singing and listened to the scrape of their footsteps and the soft rustlings of night animals scampering through the weeds.

"When are we going to stop and set up camp?" a girl asked John.

"We have to go deeper into the woods," John replied.

They kept walking. The air became colder. The trees bent and shivered around them in a swirling breeze.

"Can we set up camp now, John?" a boy asked.

"No. Deeper," John replied. "Deeper into the forest."

The path ended. The campers had to make their way through the trees, around thorny bushes, over a deep carpet of crackling dead leaves.

Owls hooted overhead. The campers heard the flutter of bat wings. Creatures scratched and slithered around their feet.

"We're really tired, John," a boy complained. "Can we stop and set up the tents?"

"Deeper into the woods," John insisted. "An overnight is no fun unless you are deep, deep in the woods."

So they kept walking. Listening to the low hoots and moans of the night animals. Watching the old trees bend and sway all around them.

Finally they stepped out into a smooth, wide clearing.

"Can we set up camp now, John?" the campers begged.

"Yes," John agreed. "We are deep in the woods now. This is the perfect place."

The campers dropped all the bags and supplies in the middle of the clearing. Silvery moonlight spilled all around them, making the smooth ground shimmer.

They pulled out the tents and started to unfold them.

But a strange sound made them all stop their work.

Ka-thump ka-thump.

"What was that?" a camper cried.

John shook his head. "Probably just the wind."

They went back to the tents. They pushed tent poles into the soft, smooth ground. They started to unfold the tents.

But the strange sound made them stop again.

Ka-thump ka-thump.

A chill of fear swept over the campers.

"What *is* that sound?" they asked.

"Maybe it's some kind of animal," John replied.

Ka-thump ka-thump.

"But it sounds so close!" a boy cried.

"It's coming from right above us," another boy said. "Or maybe beneath us!"

"It's just a noise," John told them. "Don't worry about it."

So they set up the tents. And they spread sleeping bags inside the tents.

Ka-thump ka-thump.

They tried to ignore the sound. But it was so close. So close.

And such a strange — but familiar — sound.

What could it be? the campers wondered. What on earth makes a sound like that?

Ka-thump ka thump.

The campers couldn't sleep. The noise was too loud, too frightening — too near.

Ka-thump ka-thump.

They burrowed deep into their sleeping bags. They zipped themselves in tight. They covered their ears.

Ka-thump ka-thump.

It didn't help. They couldn't escape the sound.

"John, we can't sleep," they complained.

"I can't sleep, either," John replied.

Ka-thump ka-thump.

"What should we do?" the campers asked the counselor.

John didn't get a chance to answer.

They heard another *Ka-thump ka-thump*.

And then a deep voice growled: *"WHY ARE YOU STANDING ON MY HEART?"*

The ground shook.

The campers suddenly realized what the frightening sound was. And as the ground rose up, they realized — too late — they had camped on the smooth skin of a hideous monster.

"I guess we went *too deep* into the woods!" John cried.

His last words.

Ka-thump ka-thump.

The monster's heartbeat.

And then its huge, hairy head lifted up. Its mouth pulled open. And it swallowed John and the campers without even chewing.

And as they slid down the monster's throat, the sound of the heartbeat grew louder and louder.

Ka-thump ka-thump. Ka-thump ka-thump. Ka-THUMP!

Uncle Marv shouted the last *Ka-thump* at the top of his lungs.

Some campers screamed. Some gazed at Uncle Marv in silence, their faces tight with fear. Beside me, Lucy hugged herself, biting her bottom lip.

Uncle Marv smiled, his face flickering in the dancing orange flames.

Laughing, I turned to Elvis. "That's a funny story!" I exclaimed.

Elvis narrowed his eyes at me. "Huh? Funny?"

"Yeah. It's a very funny story," I repeated.

Elvis stared hard at me. "But it's *true!*" he said softly.

8

I laughed. "Yeah. For sure," I said, rolling my eyes.

I expected Elvis to laugh. But he didn't. The firelight flickered in his pale blue eyes as he stared at me. Then he turned to talk to my brother.

A chill ran down my back. Why was he acting so weird?

Did he really think I'd believe a crazy story like that was true?

I'm twelve years old. I stopped believing in things like the Easter Bunny and the Tooth Fairy a long time ago.

I turned to Lucy. She was still hugging herself, staring intently into the fire.

"Do you believe him?" I asked, motioning to Elvis. "Is he weird or what?"

Lucy stared straight ahead. She seemed so deep in thought, I don't think she heard me.

Finally she raised her head. She blinked. "What?"

"My brother's new friend," I said, pointing to Elvis again. "He said that Uncle Marv's story was true."

Lucy nodded, but didn't reply.

"I thought it was a funny story," I said.

She picked up a twig and tossed it on the fire. I waited for her to say something. But she seemed lost in thought again.

The flames of the campfire had died down. Sparkling red embers and chunks of burning wood spread over the ground. Chris and another counselor carried fresh logs into the meeting circle.

I watched them rebuild the fire. They piled armfuls of twigs and sticks onto the burning embers. When the sticks burst into flames, the two counselors lowered logs over them.

Then they stepped back, and Uncle Marv took his place in front of the fire. He stood with his hands in the pockets of his white shorts. The full moon floated behind his head, making his long black hair shine.

He smiled. "And now I will tell the second traditional story of Camp Spirit Moon," he announced.

Once again, the circle of campers grew silent. I leaned back, trying to get my brother's attention. But Alex was staring across the fire at Uncle Marv.

Alex probably thought the first ghost story was

kind of dumb, I knew. He hates ghost stories even more than I do. He thinks they're silly baby stuff. And so do I.

So what was Elvis's problem?

Was he goofing? Just teasing me? Or was he trying to scare me?

Uncle Marv's booming voice interrupted my thoughts. "This is a story we tell every year at Camp Spirit Moon," he said. "It's the story of the Ghost Camp."

He lowered his deep voice nearly to a whisper, so that we all had to lean closer to hear him. And in hushed tones, he told us the story of the Ghost Camp.

The story takes place at a camp very much like Camp Spirit Moon. On a warm summer night, the campers and counselors met around a blazing council fire.

They roasted hot dogs and toasted marshmallows. They sang the camp songs. One of the counselors played a guitar, and he led them in singing song after song.

When they were tired of singing, the counselors took turns telling ghost stories. And telling the legends of the camp, legends that had been passed on from camper to camper for nearly a hundred years.

The evening grew late. The campfire had died

low. The moon floated high in the sky, a pale full moon.

The camp director stepped forward to end the council meeting.

Suddenly, darkness swept over the circle of campers.

They all looked up — and saw that the moon had been covered by a heavy blanket of black clouds.

And swirls of fog came drifting over the camp. A cold, wet fog. Cloudy gray at first. Then darkening.

And thickening.

Until the fog swept over the camp, billowing like black smoke.

Tumbling and swirling, the cold wet fog rolled over the dying campfire. Rolled over the campers and counselors. Over the cabins and the lake and the trees.

A choking fog, so thick and dark the campers couldn't see each other. Couldn't see the fire. Or the ground. Or the moon in the sky.

The fog lingered for a short while, swirling and tossing, low over the ground. Wet, so wet and silent.

It moved on just as silently.

Like smoke blown away.

The moonlight shone through. The grass sparkled as if a heavy dew had settled.

The fire was out. Dark purple embers sizzled over the ground.

The fog swirled away. Swept over the trees. And vanished.

And the campers sat around the dead campfire. Their eyes blank. Their arms limp at their sides.

Not moving. Not moving. Not moving.

Because they were no longer alive.

The fog had left a ghost camp in its wake.

The campers, the counselors, the camp director — they were all ghosts now.

All spirits. All ghosts. Every last one of them.

They climbed to their feet. And returned to their bunks.

They knew the ghost camp was their home now — *forever!*

With a smile, Uncle Marv stepped back from the fire.

I glanced around the circle. The faces were so solemn. No one smiled or laughed.

It's a pretty good story, I thought. Kind of scary.

But it doesn't have much of an ending.

I turned to see what Alex thought.

And gasped when I saw the terrified expression on his face. "Alex — what?" I cried, my voice cutting through the silence of the circle. "What's wrong?"

He didn't reply. His eyes were raised to the sky. He pointed up.

I gazed up too — and let out a cry of horror.

As a black, swirling fog came sweeping over the camp.

9

My mouth dropped open as I watched the fog roll closer. It darkened the ground as it moved steadily toward us.

Darkened the trees. Darkened the sky.

This is *crazy*, I told myself.

This is *impossible*!

I scooted next to Alex. "It's just a coincidence," I told him.

He didn't seem to hear me. He jumped to his feet. His whole body trembled.

I stood up beside him. "It's only fog," I said, trying to sound calm. "It gets foggy out here in the woods all the time."

"Really?" Alex asked in a tiny voice.

The black smoky fog swirled over us.

"Of course," I replied. "Hey — we don't believe in ghosts, remember? We don't think ghost stories are scary."

"But — but — " Alex stuttered. "Why is everyone staring at us?" he finally choked out.

I turned and squinted through the thick fog.

Alex was right. All around the circle, the other campers had their eyes on Alex and me. Their faces appeared to dim behind the curtain of dark mist.

"I — I don't know why they're watching us," I whispered to my brother.

Fog billowed around us. I shivered. It felt cold against my skin.

"Harry — I don't like this," Alex whispered.

The fog was so thick now, I could barely see him, even though he stood close beside me.

"I know we don't believe in ghosts," Alex said. "But I don't like this. It — it's too creepy."

From the other side of the circle, Uncle Marv's voice broke the silence. "It's a beautiful fog tonight," he said. "Let's all stand up and sing the Camp Spirit Moon song."

Alex and I were already standing. The other campers and counselors obediently climbed to their feet.

Their pale faces shimmered in and out of the fog.

I rubbed my arms. Cold and wet. I dried my face with the front of my T-shirt.

The fog grew even heavier and darker as Uncle Marv began to sing. Everyone joined in. Beside me, Alex began to sing, quieter this time.

Our voices were muffled by the heavy mist. Even Uncle Marv's booming voice sounded smaller and far away.

I tried to sing too. But I didn't know the words. And my own voice came out choked and small.

As I stared into the swirling fog, the voices faded. Everyone sang, but the sound sank into the fog.

The voices vanished. All of them. All except for Alex's.

He seemed to be the only one still singing, his voice pure and soft beside me in the dark mist.

And then Alex stopped singing, too.

The fog swept on. The darkness lifted.

Silvery moonlight washed down on us once again.

Alex and I gazed around in surprise.

No one else remained.

Alex and I were all alone. All alone in front of the dying fire.

10

I blinked. And blinked again.

I don't know what I expected. Did I think they would all appear again?

Alex and I gazed across the circle in stunned silence.

They had vanished with the fog. The campers. The counselors. Uncle Marv.

A chill ran down my back. My skin still felt damp and cold from the heavy mist.

"Wh-where — ?" Alex choked out.

I swallowed hard.

A burned log crumbled into the purple embers. The soft thud startled me.

I jumped.

And then I started to laugh.

Alex squinted at me, studying me. "Harry — ?"

"Don't you see?" I told him. "It's a joke."

He squinted at me harder. "Huh?"

"It's a camp joke," I explained. "It's a joke they probably always play on new campers here."

Alex twisted up his whole face. He was thinking about it. But I don't think he believed me.

"They all ran off into the woods," I told him. "They hid behind the fog and ran away. They were all in on the joke. I'll bet they do it to every new kid."

"But — the fog — " Alex choked out.

"I'll bet the fog was a fake!" I exclaimed. "They probably have some kind of smoke machine. To help them with the joke."

Alex rubbed his chin. I could still see the fear in his eyes.

"They probably do this all the time," I assured him. "Uncle Marv tells the story. Then somebody turns on the smoke machine. The black smoke rolls over the campfire circle. And everyone runs and hides."

Alex turned and stared into the woods. "I don't see anyone hiding back there," he said softly. "I don't see anyone watching us."

"I'll bet they're all back at the cabins," I told him. "I'll bet they're waiting for us. Waiting to see the looks on our faces."

"Waiting to laugh at us for falling for their dumb joke," Alex added.

"Let's go!" I cried. I slapped him on the shoulder. Then I started running across the wet grass toward the row of cabins.

Alex ran close behind. The moon sent a silvery path across the grass in front of us.

Sure enough — as we came near the cabins, the campers all came running out. They were laughing and hooting. Slapping each other high fives.

Enjoying their joke. A joke they play on new campers when the fog rolls in, they told us.

I saw Lucy laughing along with a bunch of girls.

Elvis grabbed Alex and wrestled him playfully to the ground.

Everyone teased us and told us how scared we looked.

"We weren't scared even for a second," I lied. "Alex and I figured it out before the fog cleared."

That made everyone start laughing and cheering all over again.

"*Owooooooooh!*"

Some of the kids cupped their hands around their mouths and made ghost howls.

"*Owooooooooh!*"

That led to more laughing and joking.

I didn't mind the teasing. Not a bit.

I felt so relieved. My heart was still pounding like crazy. And my knees felt kind of weak.

But I felt so happy that it was all a joke.

Every summer camp has its jokes, I told myself. And this is a pretty good one.

But it didn't fool me. Not for long, anyway.

"Lights Out in five minutes," Uncle Marv's booming command stopped the fun. "Lights Out, campers!"

The kids all turned and scurried to their bunks.

I stared down the row of cabins, suddenly confused. Which one was ours?

"This way, Harry," Alex said. He tugged me toward the third cabin down the path. Alex has a better memory than I do for things like that.

Elvis and two other guys were already in the cabin when Alex and I came in. They were getting changed for bed. The other guys introduced themselves. Sam and Joey.

I made my way to the bunk bed and started to undress.

"*Owooooooh!*" A ghostly howl made me jump.

I spun around and saw Joey grinning at me.

Everyone laughed. Me, too.

I like camp jokes, I thought. They're mean. But they're kind of fun.

I felt something soft and gooey under my bare foot. Yuck! I glanced down.

And saw that I had stepped in a fresh puddle of blue slime.

The cabin lights went out. But before they did, I saw blue puddles — fresh blue puddles — all over the floor.

The cold blue stuff stuck to the bottom of my foot. I stumbled through the dark cabin and found a towel to wipe it off.

What *are* these blue puddles? I asked myself as I climbed up to my top bunk.

I glimpsed Joey and Sam in the bunk against the wall.

I gasped.

They stared back at me, their eyes shining like flashlights!

What is going on here? I wondered.

What are the sticky blue puddles all over the floor?

And why do Sam and Joey's eyes glow like that in the dark?

I turned my face to the wall. I tried not to think about anything.

I had almost drifted to sleep — when I felt a cold, slimy hand sliding down my arm.

11

"Huh?"

I shot straight up. Still feeling the cold, wet touch on my skin.

I stared at my brother. "Alex — you scared me to death!" I whispered. "What do you want?"

He stood on his mattress, his dark eyes staring at me. "I can't sleep," he moaned.

"Keep trying," I told him sharply. "Why are your hands so cold?"

"I don't know," he replied. "It's cold in here, I guess."

"You'll get used to it," I said. "You always have trouble sleeping in new places."

I yawned. I waited for him to drop back onto the bottom bunk. But he didn't move.

"Harry, you don't believe in ghosts — do you?" he whispered.

"Of course not," I told him. "Don't let a couple of silly stories creep you out."

"Yeah. Right," he agreed. "Good night."

I said good night. He disappeared back to his bed. I heard him tossing around down there. He had a very squeaky mattress.

Poor guy, I thought. That dumb Ghost Camp joke with the fog really messed him up.

He'll be fine in the morning, I decided.

I turned and gazed across the dark cabin toward Joey and Sam's bunk. Were their eyes still glowing so strangely?

No.

Darkness there.

I started to turn away — then stopped.

And stared hard.

"Oh no!" I murmured out loud.

In the dim light, I could see Joey. Stretched out. Asleep.

Floating two feet above his mattress!

12

I scrambled to climb out of bed. My legs tangled in the blanket, and I nearly fell on my head!

"Hey — what's up?" I heard Alex whisper below me.

I ignored him. I swung myself around, and leaped to the floor.

"Ow!" I landed hard, twisting my ankle.

Pain shot up my leg. But I ignored it and hobbled to the door. I remembered the light switch was somewhere over there.

I had to turn on the light.

I had to see for sure that I was right. That Joey slept floating in the air above his bed.

"Harry — what's wrong?" Alex called after me.

"What's up? What time is it?" I heard Elvis groan sleepily from the bunk against the other wall.

I pulled myself across the cabin. My hand fumbled against the wall until I found the light switch.

I pushed it up.

The overhead light flashed on, flooding the tiny cabin in white light.

I raised my eyes to Joey's bunk.

He lifted his head from the pillow and squinted down at me. "Harry — what's your problem?" he asked. He was sprawled on his stomach, on top of his blanket.

Not floating in the air. Not floating.

Resting his head in his hands, yawning and staring down at me.

"Turn off the light!" Sam barked. "If Uncle Marv catches us with the light on . . ."

"But — but — " I sputtered.

"Turn it *off!*" Elvis and Sam both insisted.

I clicked off the light.

"Sorry," I muttered. "I thought I saw something."

I felt like a jerk. Why did I think I saw Joey floating in the air?

I must be as creeped out as Alex, I decided. Now I'm *seeing* things!

I scolded myself and told myself to calm down.

You're just nervous because it's your first day in a new camp, I decided.

I started slowly across the cabin to my bed. Halfway there, I stepped in a cold, sticky puddle of goo.

The next morning, Alex and I found our white Camp Spirit Moon uniforms — white shorts and

T-shirts — waiting for us at the foot of our beds.

Now we won't stand out like sore thumbs, I thought happily.

Now we can really be part of Camp Spirit Moon.

I quickly forgot about my fears from the night before. I couldn't wait for the camp day to get started.

That afternoon, Alex tried out for the Camp Spirit Moon talent show.

I had to be at the soccer field. A bunch of us were supposed to practice putting up tents. We were getting ready for an overnight in the woods.

But I stopped in front of the outdoor stage at the side of the lodge to listen to Alex sing.

A counselor named Veronica, with long, copper-colored hair all the way down her back, was in charge of the tryouts. I leaned against a tree and watched.

A lot of kids were trying out. I saw two guitar players, a boy with a harmonica, a tap dancer, and two baton twirlers.

Veronica played a small upright piano at the front of the stage. She called Alex up and asked him what song he wanted to sing.

He picked a Beatles song he likes. My brother doesn't listen to any new groups. He likes the Beatles and the Beach Boys — all the groups from ⌐ties.

₅ the only eleven-year-old I know who

listens to the oldies station. I feel kind of sorry for him. It's like he was born in the wrong time or something.

Veronica played a few notes on the piano, and Alex started to sing.

What a voice!

The other kids had all been laughing and talking and messing around. But after Alex sang for a few seconds, they got real quiet. They huddled close to the stage and listened.

He really sounded like a pro! I mean, he could probably sing with a band and make a CD.

Even Veronica was amazed. I could see her lips form the word "Wow!" as she played the piano for Alex.

When Alex finished singing, the kids all clapped and cheered. Elvis slapped Alex a high five as he hopped off the small stage.

Veronica called Elvis up next. He told her he wanted to sing an Elvis song, since he was named after Elvis Presley.

He cleared his throat and started to sing a song called "Heartbreak Hotel."

Well . . . it really *was* a heartbreak — because Elvis couldn't sing a single note on key!

Veronica tried to play along with him. But I could see that she was having trouble. I think she probably wanted to stop playing the piano and cover her ears!

Elvis had a high, scratchy voice. And the notes

came out really sour. Sour enough to make your whole face pucker up.

The kids around the stage started grumbling and walking away.

Elvis had his eyes shut. He was so wrapped up in his song, he didn't even see them!

Doesn't he know how bad he is? I wondered. Why does he want to enter a talent show when he sounds like a squealing dog?

Elvis started to repeat the chorus. I decided I had to get away from there before my eardrums popped.

I flashed Alex a thumbs-up and hurried to the soccer field.

Sam, Joey, and a bunch of other kids were already unfolding tents, getting ready for tent-raising practice. Chris, the counselor, was in charge.

He waved to me. "Harry — unroll that tent over there," he instructed. "Let's see how fast you can put it up."

I picked up the tent. It was bundled tightly, no bigger than a backpack. I turned it over in my hands. I'd never set up a tent before. I wasn't even sure how to unwrap it.

Chris saw me puzzling over it and walked over. "It's easy," he said.

lled two straps, and the nylon tent started . "See? Here are the poles. Just stretch prop it up."

He handed the bundle back to me.

"Yeah. Easy," I repeated.

"What's that noise?" Joey asked, looking up from his tent.

I listened hard. "It's Elvis singing," I told them.

The sour notes floated over the soccer field from the stage.

Sam shook his head. "It sounds like an animal caught in a trap," he said.

We all laughed.

Joey and Sam took off their sneakers and went barefoot. I took mine off, too. The warm grass felt good under my feet.

I unfolded the tent and spread it out on the grass. I piled the tent poles to the side.

The sun felt hot on the back of my neck. I slapped a mosquito on my arm.

I heard a shout and glanced up to see Sam and Joey wrestling around. They weren't fighting. They were just goofing.

They both picked up tent poles and started dueling with them, having a wild sword fight. They were laughing and having fun.

But then Sam tripped over a tent.

He lost his balance. Stumbled forward. Fell hard.

I let out a scream as the tent pole went right through his foot.

13

My stomach lurched. I felt sick.

The pointed pole had pierced the top of Sam's foot, nailing his foot to the ground.

Joey gaped, openmouthed, his eyes wide with surprise.

With a gasp, I searched for Chris. I knew Sam needed help.

Where had Chris wandered off to?

"Sam — " I choked out. "I'll get help. I'll — "

But Sam didn't cry out. He didn't react at all. Didn't even grimace.

He calmly reached down with both hands — and pulled the pole from his foot.

I let out a groan. *My* foot ached! In sympathy, I guess.

Sam tossed the pole aside.

I stared down at his foot. No cut. No blood.

It wasn't bleeding!

"Sam!" I cried. "Your foot. It's not bleeding!"

He turned and shrugged. "It missed my toes," he explained.

He dropped onto his knees and started propping up the tent.

I swallowed hard, waiting for my stomach to stop churning.

Missed his toes? I thought. Missed his *toes*?

I saw the pole sink right into his foot!

Or was I seeing things again?

For the rest of the afternoon, I tried not to think about it. I worked on the tent. Once I got it spread out, it was easy to set up.

Chris had us fold and unfold them a few times. Then we had a race to see who could set up a tent the fastest.

I won easily.

Sam said it was beginner's luck.

Chris said I was definitely ready for the overnight.

"Where do we go for the overnight?" I asked.

"Deep, deep into the woods," Chris replied. He winked at Sam and Joey.

I felt a chill, thinking about Uncle Marv's ghost story.

I shook the chill away. *No way* I was going to let myself get scared by a silly camp story.

We had instructional swim at the waterfront. The lake was clear and cold. I'm up to Junior

Lifesaver. Joey and I took turns rescuing each other.

I didn't think about Sam driving the pole through his foot. I forced it from my mind.

After the swim, I returned to the bunk to get changed for dinner. There were fresh puddles of blue goo on the cabin floor.

Nobody made a big deal about them. I didn't want to, either. So I tried hard not to think about them.

Alex came in, very excited. "I'm going to be the first act in the talent show!" he announced. "And Veronica liked my singing so much, she wants me to star in the camp musical."

"Way to go!" I cried. I slapped him a high five. Then I asked, "What about Elvis?"

"He's going to be in the show, too," Alex replied. "He's going to be stage manager."

I pulled on my white Camp Spirit Moon shorts and T-shirt and headed to the mess hall for dinner.

I saw a group of girls come out of the cabins on the other side. I searched for Lucy, but didn't see her.

I was feeling pretty good.

Not thinking about the strange things I'd seen.

Not thinking about the blue puddles of slime. The mysterious black fog.

Not thinking about the ghost story that Elvis said was true.

Not thinking about Lucy sticking her hand into the fire and pulling out my flaming hot dog.

Not thinking about Joey floating above his bed. Or Sam jamming a thick pole through his foot.

And not bleeding. Not crying out.

So totally calm about it. As if he couldn't feel it, couldn't feel any pain.

I was starving. Looking forward to dinner. Not thinking about any of these puzzling things.

Feeling really good.

But then Joey ruined my good mood at dinner. And forced all the scary thoughts back into my mind.

The food had just been served. Chicken in some kind of creamy sauce, spinach, and lumpy mashed potatoes.

I didn't care *what* it was. I was so hungry, I could eat anything!

But before I had a chance to eat, Joey called out to me from across the table. "Hey, Harry — look!"

I glanced up from my plate.

He picked up his fork — and jammed it deep into his neck!

14

"Ohhh." I let out a groan. My fork fell from my hand and clattered to the floor.

Joey grinned at me. The fork bobbed up and down, stuck in his neck.

I felt sick. My heart started to pound.

He pulled the fork out with a hard tug. His grin didn't fade. "*You* try it!" he called.

"Joey — stop it!" Elvis cried from across the table.

"Yeah. Give us a break," Sam agreed.

I stared at Joey's neck. No cut. No fork marks. No blood.

"How — how did you *do* that?" I finally stammered.

Joey's grin grew wider. "It's just a trick," he replied.

I glimpsed Alex at the end of the table. Had he seen Joey's "trick"?

Yes. Alex looked green. His mouth had dropped open in horror.

"Here. I'll show you how to do it," Joey offered.

He raised the fork again — but stopped when he saw Uncle Marv leaning over his shoulder.

"What's going on, Joey?" Uncle Marv demanded sharply.

Joey lowered the fork to the table. "Just kidding around," he replied, avoiding the camp director's hard stare.

"Well, let's eat our dinner, guys," Uncle Marv said sternly. "Without kidding around." His stubby fingers tightened over Joey's shoulders. "We have a night soccer game, you know. Boys against the girls."

Uncle Marv loosened his grip on Joey's shoulders and moved on to the next table. A food fight had broken out there. And the mashed potatoes were flying.

Joey mumbled something under his breath. I couldn't hear him over all the noise.

I turned to see how Alex was doing at the end of the table. He had his fork in his hand, but he wasn't eating. He was staring hard at Joey. My brother had a very thoughtful expression on his face.

I knew he was wondering exactly the same thing I was.

What is going on here?

Joey said the fork-stabbing was just a trick. But how did he do it? Why didn't it hurt? Why didn't he bleed?

"Night soccer games are cool!" Elvis declared. He was stuffing chicken into his mouth. The cream sauce ran down his chin.

"Especially boys against the girls," Sam agreed. "We'll *kill* them! They're pitiful."

I glanced at the girls' table across the room. They were chattering noisily. Probably about the soccer game.

I saw Lucy in the shadows near the wall. She didn't seem to be talking to anyone. She had a solemn expression on her face.

Did she keep looking over at me?

I couldn't really tell.

I ate my dinner. But my appetite had disappeared.

"How did you do that fork thing?" I asked Joey.

"I told you. It's just a trick," he replied. He turned away from me to talk to Sam.

Dessert was little squares of red, yellow, and green Jell-O. It was okay. But it needed some whipped cream.

As I was finishing my dessert, I heard some squeals from the front of the big room. I turned toward the cries — and saw a bat swooping wildly back and forth over the mess hall.

Some of the younger kids were screaming. But everyone stayed calm at my table.

The bat fluttered noisily, swooping and diving, darting from one end of the hall to the other.

Uncle Marv followed it with a broom. And after

only a minute or two, he gently pinned the bat to the wall with the straw broom head.

Then he lifted the bat off the wall, carrying it in one hand.

It was so tiny! No bigger than a mouse.

He carried it out the door and let it go.

Everyone cheered.

"That happens all the time," Sam said to me. "It's because there aren't any screens on the mess hall doors."

"And the woods are full of bats," Joey added. "Killer bats that land in your hair and suck the blood out of your head."

Sam laughed. "Yeah. Right." He grinned at me. "That's what happened to Joey. That's why he acts so weird now."

I laughed along with everyone else.

But I wondered if Sam was really joking.

I mean, Joey *did* act weird.

"Soccer field, everyone!" Uncle Marv boomed from the mess hall door. "Check with the sports counselors. Alissa and Mark will set up the teams."

Chairs scraped over the stone floor as everyone jumped up.

I saw Lucy waving to me. But Sam and Joey pulled me away.

Into a cool, cloudy night. The full moon hidden behind low clouds. The grass already wet with a heavy dew.

The counselors divided up the teams. Alex and I were on the second team. That meant we didn't play the first period. Our job was to stand on the sidelines and cheer on the boys' first team.

Two floodlights on tall poles sent down wide triangles of white light over the field. It wasn't really enough light. Long shadows spread over the field.

But that was part of the fun.

Alex stood close beside me as the game began. The girls' team scored a goal in less than a minute.

Girls on the sidelines went wild.

The players on the boys' team stood around, scratching their heads and muttering unhappily.

"Lucky break! Lucky break!" yelled Mark, a tall, lanky boys' counselor. "Go get them, guys!"

The game started up again.

The light from the floodlights appeared to dim. I raised my eyes to the sky — and saw fog rolling in.

Another swirling fog.

Mark jogged past us, looking like a big stork. "Going to be another foggy night," he said to Alex and me. "Night games are more fun in the fog." He shouted instructions to the boys' team.

The thick fog swept over us quickly, driven by a gusting wind.

Alex huddled close to me. I turned and caught his worried expression.

"Did you see what Joey did at dinner?" he asked softly.

I nodded. "He said it was a trick."

Alex thought about that for a moment. "Harry," he said, keeping his eyes on the game. "Don't you think some of these kids are a little weird?"

"Yeah. A little," I replied. I thought about the tent pole going through Sam's foot.

"Something happened at the waterfront," Alex continued. "I can't stop thinking about it."

I watched the game, squinting into the drifting fog. It was getting hard to see the players.

Cheers rang out from the girls' side. I guessed they had scored another goal. Layers of heavy fog blocked my view.

I shivered. "What happened?" I asked my brother.

"I had free swim. After tryouts for the show," he said. "There was my group and a couple of girls' groups. Younger girls, mostly."

"The lake is nice," I commented. "It's so clear and clean. And not too cold."

"Yeah. It's good," Alex agreed. He frowned. "But something strange happened. I mean — I *think* it was strange."

He took a deep breath. I could see he was really upset.

"Let's go, guys! Go, go, go!" Mark shouted to the team.

The glow from the floodlights twisted and bent in the fog, sending strange shadows over the playing field. The fog was so thick now, I had trouble telling the players from the shadows.

"I was floating on top of the water," Alex continued, wrapping his arms around his chest. "Sort of taking it easy. Moving slowly. Stroke . . . stroke . . . very slow.

"It was free swim. So we could do what we wanted. Some of the guys were having a backfloating race near the shore. But I floated out by myself.

"The water was so clear. I put my face in the water, and I stared down to the bottom. And — and I saw something down there."

He swallowed hard.

"What was it? What did you see?" I asked.

"A girl," Alex replied with a shudder. "One of the girls from the younger group. I don't know her name. She has short, curly black hair."

"She was under the water?" I demanded. "You mean, swimming underwater?"

"No." Alex shook his head. "She wasn't swimming. She wasn't moving. She was *way* underwater. I mean, near the bottom of the lake."

"She dove down?" I asked.

Alex shrugged. "I got so scared!" he cried over the shouts of the two teams. "She wasn't moving. I didn't think she was breathing. Her arms floated up and down. And her eyes — her eyes stared out blankly into the water."

"She *drowned*?" I cried.

"That's what I thought," Alex said. "I panicked. I mean, I didn't know what to do. I couldn't think. I *didn't* think. I just dove down."

"You dove down to the bottom to get her?" I asked.

"Yeah. I didn't really know if I was too late. Or if I should get a counselor. Or what," Alex said, shuddering again.

"I swam down. I grabbed her arms. Then I gripped her under the shoulders. I pulled her up. She floated up easily. Like she was weightless or something.

"I pulled her up to the surface. Then I started to drag her to the shore. I was gasping for breath. Mostly from panic, I think. My chest felt about to burst. I was so scared.

"And then I heard laughing. She laughed at me. I was still holding her under the shoulders. She turned — and spit water in my face!"

"Oh, wow!" I gasped. "Wow, Alex. You mean she was okay?"

"Yeah," Alex replied, shaking his head. "She was perfectly okay. She was laughing at me. She thought it was really funny.

"I just stared at her. I couldn't believe it. I mean, she had been way down at the bottom. For a long, long time.

"I let go of her. She floated away from me, still laughing.

"I said, 'How did you do that?' That's what I asked her. I asked, 'How long can you hold your breath?'

"And that made her laugh even harder. 'How long?' I asked.

"And she said, 'A long, long time.'

"And then she swam back to the other girls."

"And what did *you* do?" I asked Alex.

"I had to get out of the water," he replied. "I was shaking all over. I couldn't stop shaking. I — I thought . . ." His voice trailed off.

"At least she was okay," he murmured after a while. "But don't you think that was weird, Harry? And then at dinner, when Joey stuck that fork in his neck — "

"It's weird, Alex," I said softly. "But it may just be jokes."

"Jokes?" he asked. His dark eyes stared hard into mine.

"Kids always play jokes on new campers," I told him. "It's a camp tradition. You know. Terrify the new kids. It's probably just jokes. That's all."

He chewed his bottom lip, thinking about it. Even though he was standing so close to me, the swirling black fog made him appear far away.

I turned back to the game. The boys were moving across the grass toward the goal. Passing the ball, kicking it from player to player. They looked unreal, moving in and out of the swirling shadows.

Jokes, I thought.

All jokes.

I squinted into the fog. And saw something that *couldn't* be a joke.

A boy kicked the ball to the net. The girls' goalie moved to block the shot.

She wasn't fast enough. Or she stumbled.

The ball hit her smack in the forehead.

It made a sickening *thud*.

The ball bounced onto the ground.

And her head bounced beside it.

15

I gasped. And started to run.

Through the thick wisps of black fog.

The swirling, dark mist seemed to float up from the ground and sweep down from the trees. It felt cold and wet on my face as I hurtled toward the girl.

Squinting into the heavy darkness, I could see her sprawled on her stomach on the ground.

And her head . . .

Her head . . .

I bent down and grabbed it. I don't know what I was thinking.

Did I plan to plop it back on her shoulders?

In a total panic, trembling with horror, I bent into the swirling mist — and picked up the head with both hands.

It felt surprisingly hard. *Inhumanly* hard.

I raised it. Raised it close to my face.

And saw that I held a soccer ball.

Not a head. Not a girl's head.

I heard a groan. And gazed down to see the girl climb to her knees. She muttered something under her breath and shook her head.

Her head. The head on her shoulders.

She stood and frowned at me.

I stared at her face, her head. My whole body was still shaking.

"Your head — " I choked out.

She tossed back her straight blond hair. Brushed dirt off her white shorts. Then she reached for the ball.

"Harry — you're not on the first team!" I heard a boy call.

"Get off the field!" another boy demanded.

I turned and saw that the players had all gathered around.

"But I saw her head fall off!" I blurted out.

I instantly regretted it. I *knew* I shouldn't have said it.

Everyone laughed. They tossed back their heads and laughed at me. Someone slapped me on the back.

Their grinning, laughing faces floated all around me. For a moment, it looked to me as if *all* their heads had come off. I was surrounded by laughing heads, bobbing in the eerie, shadowy light from the floodlights.

The girl raised her hands to the sides of her head and tugged up. "See, Harry?" she cried. "See? It's still glued on!"

"Someone better check Harry's head!" a boy cried.

Everyone laughed some more.

A kid came up, grabbed my head, and tugged it.

"Ow!" I screamed.

More wild laughter.

I tossed the goalie the soccer ball. Then I slunk off the field.

What is *wrong* with me? I wondered. Why am I so messed up?

Why do I keep seeing things?

Am I just nervous because I'm in a new camp? Or am I totally losing it?

I trudged to the sidelines and kept walking. I didn't know where I was going. I just knew I wanted to get away from the laughing kids, away from the soccer game.

The heavy fog had settled over the field. I glanced back. I could hear the players' shouts and cheers. But I could barely see them.

I turned and started toward the row of cabins. The dew on the tall grass tickled my legs as I walked.

I was halfway to the cabins when I realized I was being followed.

.

16

I spun around.

A face floated out of the darkness.

"Alex!" I cried. In all the excitement over the soccer ball and the goalie's head, I had forgotten all about him.

He stepped close to me, so close I could see beads of sweat on his upper lip. "I saw it, too," Alex whispered.

"Huh?" I gasped. I didn't understand. "You saw *what?*"

"The girl's head," Alex said sharply. He turned back to the soccer field. To see if anyone had followed him, I guess.

Then he turned back to me and tugged my T-shirt sleeve. "I saw her head fall off, too. I saw it bounce on the ground."

I swallowed hard. "You did? Really?"

He nodded. "I thought I was going to puke. It — it was so gross."

"But — it didn't fall off!" I cried. "Didn't you

77

see? When I ran onto the field? I picked up the ball. Not her head."

"But I *saw* it, Harry," Alex insisted. "At first I thought it was just the fog. You know. My eyes playing tricks on me because of the heavy fog. But — "

"It had to be the fog," I replied quietly. "That girl — she was perfectly okay."

"But if we both saw it . . ." Alex started. He stopped and sighed. "This camp — it's so weird."

"That's for sure," I agreed.

Alex shoved his hands into the pockets of his shorts. He shook his head unhappily. "Elvis says the ghost stories are true," he said.

I put my hands on Alex's shoulders. I could feel him trembling. We don't believe in ghosts — remember?" I told him. "Remember?"

He nodded slowly.

The first howl made us both jump.

I turned to the woods. Another eerie howl rose up from the same spot.

Not an animal howl. Not an animal cry at all.

A long, mournful howl. A *human* howl.

"*Owwoooooooooooooooo.*"

Another deeper cry made me gasp.

Alex grabbed my arm. His hand felt cold as ice. "What *is* that?" he choked out.

I opened my mouth to reply — but another mournful howl interrupted.

"*Owwoooooooooooooo.*"

I heard two creatures howling. Maybe three. Maybe more.

The eerie wails floated up from behind the trees. Until it sounded as if the whole woods were howling.

Inhuman howls. *Ghostly* howls.

"We're surrounded, Harry," Alex whispered, still gripping my arm. "Whatever it is, it's got us surrounded."

17

"Owwwooooooo."

The frightening wails rose up from the trees.

"Run!" I whispered to Alex. "To the main lodge. Maybe we can find Uncle Marv. Maybe — "

Heading into the fog, we started running toward the lodge.

But the howls followed us. And grew louder.

I heard the heavy thud of footsteps behind us, tromping over the grass.

We can't escape, I realized.

Alex and I both turned at the same time.

And saw Elvis, Sam, and Joey — grinning as they ran after us.

Sam cupped his hands around his mouth and let out a long, ghostly howl. Laughing, Elvis and Joey tossed back their heads and howled too.

"You jerks!" I screamed, swinging a fist at them.

I could feel the blood rushing to my face.

I felt ready to explode. I wanted to punch those three clowns. And kick them. And pound their grinning faces.

"Gotcha!" Elvis cried. "Gotcha!" He turned to Sam and Joey. "Look at them! They're shaking! Oh, wow! They're shaking!"

Sam and Joey laughed gleefully. "Did you think there were wolves in the woods?" Sam asked.

"Or ghosts? Did you think we were ghosts?" Joey demanded.

"Shut up," I replied.

Alex didn't say a word. He lowered his eyes to the ground. I could see that he was as embarrassed as I was.

"Owwoooooo!" Elvis uttered another high-pitched howl. He threw his arms around my brother's waist and wrestled him to the ground.

"Get off! Get off!" Alex cried angrily.

The two of them wrestled around in the wet grass.

"Did I scare you?" Elvis demanded breathlessly. "Admit it, Alex. You thought it was a ghost, right? Right?"

Alex refused to reply. He let out a groan and heaved Elvis off him. They wrestled some more.

Sam and Joey stepped up beside me, grinning. Very pleased with themselves.

"You guys aren't funny," I grumbled. "That was so babyish. Really."

Joey slapped Sam a high five. "Babyish?" he cried. "If it was so babyish, why did you fall for it?"

I opened my mouth to reply — but only a choking sound came out.

Why *did* I fall for it? I asked myself.

Why did I let myself get scared by three guys standing behind trees and making howling sounds?

Normally, I would have laughed at such a dumb joke.

As the five of us walked to the cabin, I thought hard about it. The campers and counselors had all been trying to scare Alex and me since we arrived, I realized. Even Uncle Marv had tried to scare us with his creepy stories.

They must have a tradition of trying to scare new campers at Camp Spirit Moon, I decided.

And it works. It really has scared Alex and me. It has made us tense. Jumpy. Ready to leap out of our skins at the slightest noise.

We stepped into the cabin. I clicked the light on.

Elvis, Sam, and Joey were still laughing, still enjoying their joke.

Alex and I have got to get it together, I decided.

We've got to shove all the stupid stuff about ghosts out of our heads.

We don't believe in ghosts, I told myself.

We don't believe in ghosts. We don't believe in ghosts.

I repeated that sentence over and over. Like a chant.

Alex and I don't believe in ghosts. We've never believed in ghosts.

Never. Never.

One night later . . . after a short hike through the woods — I *did* believe in ghosts!

18

Alex and I took a lot of teasing the next day.

Coming out of the mess hall after breakfast, someone tossed a soccer ball at me and screamed, "My head! Give me back my head!"

We had instructional swim in the morning. Joey and Sam and some of the other guys started howling like ghosts. Everyone thought it was a riot.

I saw Lucy hanging out on the shore with some girls from her cabin. The other girls were laughing at the ghostly howls. Lucy was the only one who didn't laugh.

In fact, she had a solemn expression on her face. A thoughtful expression.

Several times, I caught her staring at me.

She's probably thinking about what a total baby I am, I told myself unhappily. I'll bet she feels sorry for me. Because I acted like such a jerk in front of everyone on the soccer field last night.

After instructional swim, I dried myself off.

Then I wrapped the towel around myself and walked over to Lucy at the little boat dock.

The other girls had wandered away. Lucy stood in her white shorts and T-shirt. She had one foot on a plastic canoe, making it bob up and down in the shallow water.

"Hi," I said. I suddenly realized I didn't know what to say.

"Hi," she replied.

She didn't smile. Her dark eyes locked on mine.

To my surprise, she turned quickly — and ran off.

"Hey — !" I called. I started to run after her. But stopped when my legs got tangled in my towel. "Hey — what's your problem?"

She vanished behind the Arts and Crafts cabin. She never looked back.

I *know* what her problem is, I told myself sadly. She doesn't want to be seen talking to a total nutcase. To someone who thinks that a girl's head can roll off. And who thinks there are howling ghosts lurking in the woods.

I wrapped the towel around me. Sam and Joey and some other guys were staring at me from the shore. I could see by the grins on their faces that they had seen Lucy run away from me.

"Maybe it's your breath!' Joey teased.

They all fell on the ground, howling.

*   *   *

After lunch, we had letter-writing time. The counselors made sure we all stayed in our bunks and wrote letters home to our parents.

It was a camp rule that we had to write home once a week. "So your parents won't worry about you," Uncle Marv announced at lunch. "We want them to know that you're having the best summer of your lives — right?"

"Yohhhhhhhhhh, Spirits!" everyone cheered.

I wasn't exactly having the best summer of my life.

In fact, so far, this was one of the worst.

But I decided not to write that in my letter home.

I climbed up to my top bunk and started to think about my letter to Mom and Dad.

Please come and get me, I thought I might write.

Everyone is weird here. Alex and I are both scared out of our wits.

No. No way. I couldn't write that.

I leaned over the side of the mattress and peered down at my brother. He was sitting on his bunk, crouched over his letter. I could see him scribbling away.

"What are you writing?" I called down.

"I'm telling them about the Camp Spirit Moon talent show," he replied. "How I'm going to be the star. And how I'm going to be in the musical next week."

"Nice," I muttered.

I decided I'd tell my parents only good things, too. Why worry them? Why make them think that I'm losing it?

If Alex isn't writing about all the weird things, I won't either, I decided.

I leaned over my sheet of paper and started my letter:

Dear Mom and Dad,

Camp Spirit Moon is a lot more exciting than I ever dreamed. . . .

"Tonight's after-dinner activity is a night hike," Uncle Marv announced.

A cheer shook the wooden rafters of the huge mess hall.

"Where are we going to hike?" someone called out.

Uncle Marv grinned. "Deep, deep into the woods."

Of course, that answer reminded everyone of Uncle Marv's ghost story. Some kids cheered. Others laughed.

Alex and I exchanged glances.

But the hike turned out to be fun. A full moon made the woods glow. We followed a path that curved around the lake.

Everyone seemed in a good mood. We sang the camp song so many times, I almost learned the words!

About halfway around the lake, two deer stepped out onto the path. A mother and her doe.

The little one was so cute. It looked just like Bambi.

The two deer stared at us. They turned up their noses, as if to say, "What are *you* doing in *our* woods?"

Then they calmly loped into the trees.

The path headed through a small, round clearing. As we stepped out of the trees, the ground appeared to light up. The moonlight poured down so brightly, I felt as if I could see every bush, every weed, every blade of grass.

It was really awesome.

I started to relax. Sam, Joey, and I walked along singing, making up funny words to songs we knew. We sang "On Top of Spaghetti" about twenty times — until kids *begged* us to stop singing it!

Why have I been so crazy? I asked myself.

I've made some cool new friends here at Camp Spirit Moon. I'm having an excellent time.

I felt great until we returned to camp.

The black fog had started to roll in. It greeted us, wrapping its cold, wet mists around us, darkening the sky, the ground, the whole camp.

"Lights Out in ten minutes," Uncle Marv announced.

Kids scampered to their cabins.

But two strong arms held me from behind. Held me back.

"Hey — !" I cried out. I felt myself being pulled into the trees.

"Ssshhhhh," someone whispered in my ear.

I spun around to find Lucy holding onto me. "What are you doing?" I whispered. "We have to go to our bunks. We have to get ready for — "

"Ssshhhhhh," she hissed again in my ear.

Her dark eyes searched my face. Were those tears staining her pale cheeks?

Clouds of fog rolled around us.

She loosened her grip on my arms. But her eyes stayed on mine. "Harry, you've got to help me," she whispered.

I swallowed hard. "Lucy, what's wrong?"

"I think you know," she said softly. "It's all true. What you think. It's true."

I didn't understand. I stared back at her with my mouth open.

"We're ghosts, Harry," Lucy told me. "We're all ghosts at this camp."

"But, Lucy — " I started.

"Yes." She nodded sadly. "Yes. Yes. Yes. I'm a ghost too."

19

The trees disappeared behind the fog. The moon-light made Lucy's eyes sparkle like dark jewels. But the light faded from her eyes as the fog covered the moon.

I didn't blink. I didn't move. I suddenly felt as wooden as the trees hiding behind the swirling fog.

"You — you're joking, right?" I stammered. "This is one of those great Camp Spirit Moon jokes?"

But I knew the answer.

I could read the answer in her dark eyes. In her trembling mouth. In her pale, pale skin.

"I'm a ghost," she repeated sadly. "The stories — they're true, Harry."

But I don't believe in ghosts!

That's what I almost blurted out.

But how could I not believe in ghosts when one stood right in front of me, staring into my face?

How could I not believe in Lucy?

"I believe you," I whispered.

She sighed. She turned her face away.

"How did it happen?" I asked.

"Just as Uncle Marv told in the story," she replied. "We were sitting around the campfire. All of us. Just like the other night. The fog rolled in. Such a dark, heavy fog."

She sighed again. Even in the darkness, I could see the tears glistening in her eyes.

"When the fog finally floated away," Lucy continued, "we were all dead. All ghosts. We've been out here ever since. I can't explain any more. I don't know any more."

"But — when did it happen?" I demanded. "How long . . . how long have you been a ghost, Lucy?"

She shrugged. "I don't know. I've lost track of time. There *is* no time when you're a ghost. There's just one day and then the next. And then the next. Forever, I guess."

I stared at her without speaking.

Chill after chill swept down my back. My whole body was shaking. I didn't even try to stop it.

I reached out and grabbed her hand.

I guess I wanted to see if she was real or not. One last test to see if she was pulling a joke.

"Oh!" I dropped her hand as its icy cold shot through me. So cold. Her hand — as cold as the black fog.

"You believe me now?" she asked softly. Once again her dark eyes studied my face.

I nodded. "I — I believe you," I stammered. "I believe you, Lucy."

She didn't reply.

I could still feel the cold of her hand on my fingers.

"The blue puddles," I murmured. "The sticky blue puddles on the cabin floor. Do you know what they are?"

"Yes," she replied. "Those puddles are drops of protoplasm."

"Huh? Protoplasm?"

She nodded. "The puddles are made when we materialize. When we make ourselves visible."

She twisted her face into a sorrowful frown. "It takes so much strength to make ourselves visible. So much energy. The protoplasm puddles are made when we use that energy."

I didn't really understand.

But I knew when I stepped in them that the slimy blue puddles were something strange. Something inhuman.

Traces of ghosts.

"And the things Alex and I saw?" I demanded. "Kids floating above their bunks? Their eyes glowing like spotlights? Kids stabbing themselves and not bleeding? Not crying out in pain?"

"Some of the kids tried to scare you," Lucy confessed. "They only wanted a little fun, Harry.

It isn't fun being a ghost. Believe me. It isn't fun spending day after day after day out here, knowing you aren't real anymore. Knowing you will never grow. Knowing you will never change." She uttered a loud sob from deep in her chest. "Knowing you will never have a *life!*"

"I — I'm so sorry," I stammered.

Her expression changed.

Her eyes narrowed. Her mouth twisted into an unpleasant sneer.

I took a step back, suddenly afraid.

"Help me, Harry," Lucy whispered. "I can't stand it anymore. You've got to help me get away from here."

"Get away?" I cried, taking another step back. "How?"

"You've got to let me possess your mind," Lucy insisted. "You've got to let me take over your body!"

20

"No!" I gasped.

Panic shot through my body. I felt every muscle tense. The blood throbbed at my temples.

"I need to take over your mind, Harry," Lucy repeated, stepping toward me. "Please. Please help me."

"No!" I uttered again.

I wanted to turn and run. But I couldn't move. My legs felt like Jell-O. My whole body shook.

I don't believe in ghosts.

That thought flashed into my mind.

But it wasn't true anymore.

I stood at the edge of the woods — staring at Lucy. Staring at Lucy's ghost.

The fog swept around us.

Again, I tried to run. But my legs wouldn't cooperate.

"Wh-what do you want to do to me?" I finally choked out. "Why do you have to take over my mind?"

"It's my only way to escape," Lucy replied. Her eyes locked on mine. "My only way."

"Why don't you just run away?" I demanded.

She sighed. "If I try to leave the camp by myself, I'll disappear. If I try to leave the others, I'll fade away. I'll join the mist, be part of the fog."

"I — I don't understand," I stammered.

I took a step back. The fog seemed to tighten around me, cold and wet.

Lucy stood two feet in front of me. But I could barely see her. She seemed to shimmer in and out with the fog.

"I need help." Her voice floated softly. I had to struggle to hear her. "The only way a ghost can escape is to take over the mind of a living person."

"But — that's *impossible!*" I screeched.

What a dumb thing to say, I scolded myself. *Seeing a ghost* is impossible! *Everything* happening to me is impossible.

But it's happening.

"I need to possess the mind and body of a living boy or girl," Lucy explained. "I need to take over your body, Harry. I need you to take me away from here."

"No!" I screamed again. "I can't! I mean . . ." My heart thudded so hard, I could barely speak.

"I can't let you take over my mind," I finally managed to say. "If you do that, I won't be *me* anymore."

I started to back away.

I have to get to the cabin, I decided. I have to get Alex. We have to run away from this camp. As fast as we can.

"Don't be scared," Lucy pleaded. She followed me. The fog circled us, as if holding us inside.

"Don't be scared," Lucy said. "As soon as we are far away from here, I'll get out. I'll leave your mind. I'll leave your body. I promise, Harry. As soon as we escape this camp, I'll go away. You will be yourself again. You will be perfectly okay."

I stopped backing up. My whole body trembled. The fog washed its cold mist over me.

"Please, Harry," Lucy begged. "Please. I promise you'll be okay. I promise."

I squinted at her through the rising mists.

Should I do it?

Should I let Lucy take over my mind?

Will she give it back?

Can I believe her?

21

Lucy floated in front of me. Her dark eyes pleaded with me. "Please," she whispered.

"No. I'm sorry. I can't." The words escaped my lips almost before I thought them. "I can't, Lucy."

She shut her eyes. I could see the muscles in her jaw tighten as she gritted her teeth.

"I'm sorry," I repeated, backing up.

"I'm sorry too," she said coldly. Her eyes narrowed. Her lips formed a sneer. "I'm really sorry, Harry. But you don't have a choice. You *have* to help me!"

"No! No way!"

I turned and tried to run.

But something held me back. The fog. It tightened around me.

The thick, wet mist. A choking mist. It drew around me, pushing me, holding me in place.

I tried to scream for help. But the fog muffled my cry.

Lucy vanished behind the black fog.

And then I felt something cold on the top of my head.

My hair tingled.

I reached up with both hands. And felt ice. As if a frost had settled over my hair.

"No!" I screamed. "Lucy — no!"

The cold sank down. My scalp itched. My face froze.

I rubbed my cheeks.

Numb.

Cold and numb.

"Lucy — please!" I begged.

I could feel her — so light, so cold — settling into my body. Sinking into my brain.

I could feel her. And I could feel myself slipping away.

Slipping . . . slipping . . .

As if drifting into a deep sleep.

The cold spreading over me. Sweeping down my neck. Down my chest.

"Nooooo!" I uttered a long howl of protest.

I shut my eyes tight. I knew I had to concentrate. I had to think hard. I had to keep awake. I couldn't let myself fade away.

I couldn't let her take over.

I couldn't let her shove my mind aside. And take control. Take control of my body.

I set my jaw hard. And kept my eyes shut. And tightened every muscle.

No! I thought. *No — you can't do this to me, Lucy!*

You can't take my mind!

You can't take over. You can't — because I won't let you!

The cold settled over me. My skin tingled. I felt numb all over.

And so sleepy . . . so sleepy . . .

22

"Nooooo!" I tossed back my head in another long howl.

If I can keep screaming, I can keep awake, I told myself.

And I can fight Lucy off. I can force her away.

"Noooooooo!" I wailed into the spinning, whirling fog.

"Noooooooo!"

And I felt the cold start to lift.

"Noooooo!"

I squeezed my arms. Rubbed my cheeks. And knew the feeling was returning.

"Nooooooo!"

I suddenly felt lighter. And totally alert.

I did it! I realized. I fought her off!

But how long did I have before she tried to take over again?

I took a deep breath. Then another.

I'm breathing, I told myself. I'm me — and I'm breathing.

I felt stronger now. I lowered my head and darted into the fog.

My sneakers pounded the ground. I made my way to the cabin.

The lights were out. The other guys were in their bunks.

I burst inside and let the screen door slam behind me.

"What's up?" Sam demanded.

I didn't answer him. I ran across the room. Grabbed my brother. Shook him hard. "Come on. Hurry," I ordered.

"Huh?" Alex squinted up at me sleepily.

I didn't say another word. I tossed him his shorts and his sneakers.

I heard the other guys stirring. Joey sat up in his bed. "Harry — where *were* you?" he asked.

"Lights Out was ten minutes ago," Sam said. "You're going to get us all in trouble."

I ignored them. "Alex — hurry!" I whispered.

As soon as he had his sneakers tied, I grabbed his arm and tugged him to the door. "Harry — what's wrong?" he asked.

"Where are you two going?" I heard Joey call.

I pulled Alex outside. The screen door slammed behind us.

"Run!" I cried. "I'll explain later. We have to get out of here — now!"

"But, Harry — "

I pulled Alex over the grass. The fog had parted

enough to let a trail of moonlight slip through. We followed the trail to the woods.

Our sneakers slipped and slid over the wet grass. The only other sound was the chirp of crickets and the rush of wind rattling the pine trees.

After a minute or two, Alex wanted to stop to catch his breath.

"No," I insisted. "Keep moving. They'll follow us. They'll find us."

"Where are we going?" Alex demanded.

"Deep into the woods," I told him. "As far away from that camp as we can."

"But I can't keep running, Harry," Alex cried. "My side hurts and — "

"They're all ghosts!" I blurted out. "Alex — I know you won't believe me — but you've got to try. The kids. The counselors. Uncle Marv. They're all ghosts!"

Alex's expression grew solemn. "I know," he replied in a tiny voice.

"Huh? How do you know?" I demanded.

We squeezed between two tangled tree trunks. Over the chirp of crickets, I could hear the lake washing over the shore just beyond some tall shrubs.

We're still too close to the camp, I told myself.

I pulled my brother in the other direction. Away from the lake. Pushing aside tall weeds and shrubs, we made our own path, deeper into the woods.

"Alex — how do you know?" I repeated.

"Elvis told me," he replied, wiping sweat off his forehead with his arm.

We ducked under a tall thorn bush. Thorns scraped the top of my head. I ignored the pain and kept moving.

"Elvis said the ghost story about the fog was true," Alex continued. "I thought he was just trying to scare me. But then he — he — " Alex's voice trailed off.

We ran into a small clearing. Moonlight made the grass glow like silver. My eyes flashed in one direction, then the other. I couldn't decide which way to run.

I swatted a mosquito off my arm. "What did Elvis do?" I asked Alex.

Alex raked back his dark hair. "He tried to take over my mind," he told me in a trembling voice. "He floated into the fog. And then I started to feel really cold."

Twigs snapped. Dry leaves crackled.

Footsteps?

I shoved Alex back into the trees. Out of the clearing.

We pressed against a wide tree trunk and listened.

Silence now.

"Maybe it was a squirrel, or a chipmunk, or something," Alex whispered.

"Maybe," I replied, listening hard.

Moonlight trickled through the treetops. It made shadows dance over the smooth clearing.

"We have to keep going," I said. "We're still too close to the camp. If the ghosts follow us . . ."

I didn't finish my thought. I didn't want to *think* about what would happen if the ghosts followed us. If they caught us . . .

"Which way is the highway?" Alex asked, his eyes searching the trees. "It isn't too far from the camp — right? If we can get to the highway, someone will give us a ride."

"Good idea," I said. Why hadn't I thought of that?

Now here we were, in the middle of the woods. Far from the highway.

I didn't even know which direction to go to find it.

"It must be back that way," Alex suggested, pointing.

"No. That's the way back to the camp," I argued.

Alex started to reply — but a loud thumping sound made him stop. "Did you hear that?" he whispered.

I did.

And then I heard it again.

A loud thump. Very close by.

"Is it an animal?" I cried softly.

"I — I don't think so," Alex stammered.

KA-THUMP.

Louder.

Is it a ghost? I wondered.

Has one of them found us?

"Quick — this way!" I urged. I grabbed Alex by the wrist and tugged him hard.

We had to get away from whatever was making that frightening noise.

KA-THUMP.

Louder.

"We're going the wrong way!" I cried.

We spun around and darted back into the clearing.

KA-THUMP.

"Which way?" Alex screeched. "Which way? It — it's *everywhere!*"

KA-THUMP.

And then — from somewhere just ahead of us — a deep, booming voice growled, *"WHY ARE YOU STANDING ON MY HEART?"*

23

The ground tumbled and shook.

Alex and I both let out terrified cries.

But our cries were drowned out by a rumbling sound that quickly rose to a roar.

The ground gave way beneath us.

We both raised our arms high as we toppled over.

I landed on my hands and knees. Alex fell onto his back. The ground trembled and tossed, tumbling us around.

"It — it's the *monster*!" Alex shrieked.

But that's impossible! I thought, struggling to my feet.

That monster is from a story. A dumb camp ghost story.

It can't be here in the woods.

I helped pull Alex up. But the ground shook again, and we both fell to our knees.

KA-THUMP. KA-THUMP.

"It can't be real!" I cried. "It can't — "

My mouth dropped open in horror as a huge, hairy head raised itself in front of us. Its eyes glowed as red as flames — round, terrifying, glowing eyes set deep in an ugly, growling face. The creature glared furiously at us.

"Th-the monster!" Alex stuttered.

We were both on our knees, bouncing helplessly on the rolling, tossing ground.

Was it the ground? Or the monster's chest?

The creature opened an enormous cavern of a mouth. It flashed rows and rows of jagged yellow teeth.

Slowly it raised its head, moving closer. Closer.

Opening its hairy jaws wide. Preparing to swallow us as we frantically struggled to scramble away.

"Harry — ! Harry — !" Alex shrieked my name. "It's going to eat us! It's going to swallow us whole!"

And then — in a flash — I had an idea.

24

The huge monster uttered a low growl.

Its hairy mouth opened wider. An enormous purple tongue rolled out. I gasped when I saw that the tongue was covered in prickly burrs.

"Look out, Alex!" I cried.

Too late.

The ground tossed, bouncing us both into the air. We landed with a hard *plop* on the tongue.

"Owwww!" we both howled. It felt like a cactus!

Slowly, the prickly purple tongue began to slide, carrying us into the creature's open mouth.

"We don't believe in monsters," I told Alex.

I had to shout over the bellowing of the hungry monster. The tongue carried us closer. Closer to the rows of jagged yellow teeth.

"We don't believe in this monster!" I shouted. "It is just made up. Part of a story. If we don't believe in it, it can't exist!"

Alex's whole body shook. He hunched over,

making himself into a tight ball. "It looks pretty real!" he choked out.

The tongue dragged us closer. I could smell the monster's foul breath. I could see black stains on its jagged teeth.

"Concentrate," I instructed my brother. "We don't believe in you. We don't believe in you."

Alex and I began chanting those words, over and over.

"We don't believe in you. We don't believe in you."

The purple tongue carried us into the huge mouth. I tried to grab onto the teeth. But they were too slippery.

My hands slid off. I felt myself being swallowed. Down, down. Into sour darkness.

"We don't believe in you. We don't believe in you." Alex and I continued to chant.

But our voices were muffled as we slid down the creature's throbbing throat.

"Harry — it *swallowed* us!" Alex wailed.

"Keep chanting," I ordered him. "If we don't believe in it, it *can't* exist!"

"We don't believe in you. We don't believe in you."

A glob of thick saliva rolled over me. I gagged as it clung to my clothes, my skin — hot and sticky.

The walls of the throat throbbed harder.

Pulling us down. Down.

Down into the vast, churning gurgling pit of a stomach below.

"Ohhhh." Alex let out a long, defeated sigh. He sank to his knees. He was covered in thick saliva too.

"Keep chanting! It's got to work! It's got to!" I screamed.

"We don't believe in you. We don't believe in you."

"We don't believe in you!"

Alex and I both opened our mouths in screams of horror as we began to fall.

Falling, falling, into the churning stomach below.

25

I shut my eyes.

And waited for the splash. Waited for the crash.

Waited to hit the stomach floor.

Waited.

When I opened my eyes, I was standing on the ground. Standing next to Alex in a grassy clearing.

The pine trees shivered in the breeze. A full moon poked out from behind wispy clouds.

"Hey — !" I cried. I was so happy to hear my own voice!

So happy to see the sky. The ground. So happy to breathe the cool air.

Alex started spinning. Spinning like a top. Laughing at the top of his lungs. "We didn't believe in you!" he cried gleefully. "We didn't believe in you — and it *worked*!"

We were both so thrilled. So excited that the monster had vanished.

Poof! A puff of imagination.

I started to spin with Alex. Spinning and laughing.

We stopped when we realized we were no longer alone.

I let out a startled cry when I saw the faces all around us. The pale, pale faces with their glowing eyes.

I recognized Sam, and Joe, and Lucy, and Elvis.

I moved close to Alex as the campers — the ghost campers — moved to form a circle around us. To trap us.

Uncle Marv moved into the circle. His tiny eyes glowed red as fire. He narrowed them angrily at Alex and me.

"Capture them!" he bellowed. "Take them back to camp. No one ever escapes Camp Spirit Moon."

Several counselors moved quickly to grab us.

We couldn't move. There was nowhere to run.

"What are you going to *do* to us?" I cried.

26

"We need living kids," Uncle Marv boomed. "We cannot allow living kids to escape. Unless they carry one of us with them."

"Noooo!" Alex wailed. "You can't take over my mind! You can't! I won't let you!"

The ghostly circle tightened. The ghost campers moved in on us.

I tried to stop my legs from shaking. Tried to slow my pounding heart.

"Alex — we don't believe in *them*, either," I whispered.

He stared at me, confused for a moment. Then he understood.

We made the monster vanish by not believing in him. We could do the same thing to the ghost campers.

"Grab them. Take them back to camp," Uncle Marv ordered the counselors.

"We don't believe in you. We don't believe in you," Alex and I started to chant.

"We don't believe in you. We don't believe in you."

I stared hard at the circle of ghostly faces. Waited for them to disappear.

I chanted with my brother. Chanted faster. Chanted louder.

"We don't believe in you. We don't believe in you."

I shut my eyes. Shut them tight.

And when I opened them . . .

The ghosts were still there.

"You can't make us disappear, Harry," Lucy said, stepping into the circle. She narrowed her eyes at me. They glittered cold and silvery in the moonlight.

"You made the monster disappear because it wasn't real, just one of our ghost tricks," Lucy explained. "We made you see it. But we're all real! All of us! And we're not going to vanish in a puff of smoke."

"We're not going away," Elvis added, moving close to my brother. "In fact, we're coming closer. A lot closer."

"I'm taking over your mind," Lucy whispered to me. "I'm going to escape Camp Spirit Moon inside your mind and body."

"Nooo! No — please!" I protested.

I tried to back up. But the other ghost campers had me trapped.

"You can't! I won't let you!" I shrieked to Lucy, frozen in terror.

"Go away!" Alex shouted at Elvis.

The woods darkened as clouds swept over the moon. All around me, the ghostly eyes appeared to glow brighter.

I saw Elvis reach for my brother.

And then my view was blocked by Lucy. She floated up. Up off the ground. Up over me.

"No! Stay away! Stay away!" I screamed.

But I felt my hair tingle.

I felt the cold sweep down over me. Down, down.

I felt Lucy's ghostly cold. Felt her slipping into my mind.

Slipping down, down. Taking over.

And I knew I couldn't escape.

27

"Get away, Lucy. I'm going first!" I heard a voice shout.

"No way!" a boy cried. "Move out of the way. Uncle Marv said I could be first!"

I could feel the cold sweep up from my body. I opened my eyes — and saw Lucy back on the ground.

Other kids tugged her away.

"Let go of me!" Lucy screamed, pulling back. "I saw him first!"

"Finders keepers!" another ghostly girl cried.

They are fighting over me, I realized.

They pulled Lucy away. And now they're fighting to see who will take over my mind.

"Hey — let go!" I heard a ghostly girl cry. I saw her wrestling with another girl.

The ghosts were wrestling and fighting, shoving and clawing at each other. I saw the counselors join the fight.

"Stop this! Stop this!" Uncle Marv bellowed.

He tried to pull the fighting campers apart.

But they ignored him and continued to battle.

And as I stared in horror, they began to spin around me. Faster and faster. A ghostly circle of wrestling, fighting, shrieking campers. Boys and girls, counselors and Uncle Marv, spinning, struggling, clawing.

Faster. Faster.

They spun around and around my brother and me.

Until they became a swirl of white light.

And then the light faded. Faded to gray smoke.

Wisps of smoke that floated to the trees. And disappeared in the trembling branches.

Alex and I stood watching until the last wisp of smoke had floated away.

"They're gone," I choked out. "They fought each other. And they're gone. All of them."

I shook my head. I drew in a deep breath of fresh air.

My heart was still pounding. My whole body trembled.

But I was okay. Alex and I were okay.

"Are they really gone?" Alex asked in a tiny voice.

"Yes. Let's go," I said, taking his arm. "Come on. Hurry. Let's get away from here."

He followed me eagerly. "Where are we going?"

"To the highway," I said. "We'll walk past the camp to the highway. And we'll stop the first car that comes by. We'll get to a phone. We'll call Mom and Dad."

I slapped my brother on the back. "We'll be okay, Alex!" I cried happily. "We'll be home before you know it!"

We walked quickly through the woods. Pushing bushes and weeds out of the way. Making our own path.

As we made our way to the highway, Alex started to hum a song to himself.

"Whoa!" I cried. "Alex, what's wrong?"

"Huh?" He stared at me in surprise.

I stopped and held him in place. "Sing that again," I ordered.

He sang a little more.

Horrible! His singing was horrible. Totally off-key and sour.

I stared hard into my brother's eyes. "Elvis — is that *you* in there?" I cried.

Elvis's voice came out of Alex's mouth. "Please, Harry, don't tell," he begged. "I *swear* I'll never sing again — if you promise not to tell!"

Add *more*

Goosebumps®

to your collection . . .

Here's a chilling preview of

HOW TO KILL A MONSTER

"That's their house," Dad insisted as the car bumped up a narrow sandy road. "That's Grandma and Grandpa's house."

"That *can't* be their house." Clark rubbed his eyes. "It's a swamp mirage. I read about them in *Creatures from the Muck*. The swamp mud plays tricks on your eyes. It makes you see things."

See what I mean about Clark? He really does believe the stuff he reads.

And it was beginning to sound right to me, too. How else could you explain Grandma and Grandpa's house?

A castle.

A castle in the middle of a swamp.

Almost hidden in a grove of dark, towering trees.

Dad pulled the car up to the front door. I stared at the house in the glow of the headlights.

Three stories high. Built of dark gray stone. A turret rose up on the right side. On the left, a sliver of white smoke curled from a blackened chimney.

"I thought swamp houses were smaller," I murmured, "and built on stilts."

"That's the way they look in my comic," Clark agreed. "And what's with the windows?" His voice shook. "Are they vampires or something?"

I stared at the windows. They were tiny. And I could see only three of them. Three tiny windows in the entire house. One on each floor.

"Come on, kids," Mom said. "Let's get your luggage."

Mom, Dad, and Clark climbed out of the car and headed for the trunk. I stood by the car door with Charley.

The night air felt cold and damp on my skin.

I stared up.

Up at the big dark house. Almost hidden behind the trees. In the middle of nowhere.

And then I heard the howl. A mournful howl. From somewhere deep in the swamp.

A chill swept through me.

Charley pressed against my leg. I bent to pet him. "What could that be?" I whispered to the dog in the dark. "What kind of creature howls like that?"

"Gretchen. Gretchen." Mom waved from the front door of the house. Everyone else had gone inside.

"Oh, my," Grandma said as I stepped into the

dim entrance. "This can't be our little Gretchen." She wrapped her frail arms around me and gave me a big hug.

She smelled just the way I had remembered — musty. I glanced at Clark. He rolled his eyes.

I stepped back and forced a smile.

"Move aside, Rose," Grandpa yelled. "Let me get a look at her."

"He's a little hard-of-hearing," Dad whispered to me.

Grandpa clasped my hand between his wrinkled fingers. He and Grandma seemed so slight. So fragile.

"We're really happy you're here!" Grandma exclaimed. Her blue eyes twinkled. "We don't get many visitors!"

"For a while, we thought you weren't coming," Grandpa shouted. "We expected you hours ago."

"Flat tire," Dad explained.

"Tired?" Grandpa wrapped his arms around Dad. "Well, then come in and sit down, son."

Clark giggled. Mom shoved an elbow into his side. Grandpa and Grandma led us into the living room.

The room was enormous. Our whole house could probably fit inside it.

The walls were painted green. Drab green. I stared up at the ceiling. Up at an iron chandelier that held twelve candles, in a circle.

An enormous fireplace took up most of one wall.

The other walls were covered with black-and-white photographs. Yellowed with age.

Photographs everywhere. Of people I didn't recognize. Probably dead relatives, I thought.

I glanced through a doorway into the next room. The dining room. It appeared to be as big as the living room. Just as dark. Just as dreary.

Clark and I sat down on a tattered green couch. I felt the old springs sag under my weight. Charley groaned and stretched out on the floor at our feet.

I glanced around the room. At the pictures. At the worn rug. At the shabby tables and chairs. The flickering light high above us made our shadows dance on the dark walls.

"This place is creepy," Clark whispered. "And it really smells bad — worse than Grandma and Grandpa."

I choked back a laugh. But Clark was right. The room smelled strange. Damp and sour.

Why do two old people want to live like this? I wondered. In this musty, dark house. Deep in the swamp.

"Would anyone like something to drink?" Grandma interrupted my thoughts. "How about a nice cup of tea?"

Clark and I shook our heads no.

Mom and Dad also said no. They sat opposite us. The stuffing in their chairs spilled out the backs.

"Well, you're finally here!" Grandpa yelled to us. "It's just great. So, tell me — how come you were late?"

"Grandpa," Grandma shouted to him, "no more questions!" Then she turned to us. "After such a long trip, you must be starving. Come into the kitchen. I made my special chicken pot pie — just for you."

We followed Grandma and Grandpa into the kitchen. It looked like all the other rooms. Dark and dingy.

But it didn't smell as ancient as the other rooms. The tangy aroma of chicken pot pie floated through the air.

Grandma removed eight small pies from the oven. One for each of us — and a couple of extras in case we were starving, I guessed.

Grandma placed one on my plate, and I began to dig right in. I *was* starving.

As I lifted the fork to my mouth, Charley sprang up from his place on the floor and started to sniff.

He sniffed our chairs.

The counter.

The floor.

He leaped up to the table and sniffed.

"Charley, stop!" Dad ordered. "Down!"

Charley jumped from the table. Then he reared up in front of us — and curled his upper lip.

He let out a growl.

A low, menacing growl that erupted into loud barking.

Furious barking.

"What on earth is wrong with him?" Grandma demanded, frowning at the dog.

"I don't know," Dad told her. "He's never done that before."

"What is it, Charley?" I asked. I shoved my chair from the table and approached him.

Charley sniffed the air.

He barked.

He sniffed some more.

A chill of fear washed over me.

"What is it, boy? What do you smell?"

5

I grabbed Charley's collar. Petted him. Tried to calm him down. But he jerked out of my grasp.

He barked even louder.

I reached for his collar again and tugged him toward me. His nails scraped the floor as he pulled away.

The more I tugged on his collar, the harder Charley fought. He swung his head sharply from side to side. And started to growl.

"Easy, boy," I said softly. "Eeea — sy."

Nothing worked.

Finally Clark helped me drag Charley into the living room — where he started to settle down.

"What do you think is wrong with him?" Clark asked as we stroked the dog's head.

"I don't know." I stared down at Charley. Restless now, he turned in circles. Then he sat. Then turned in circles. Again and again.

"I just don't get it. He's never done that before. Ever."

Clark and I decided to wait in the living room with Charley while Mom and Dad finished eating. We weren't hungry anymore.

"How's that dog of yours?" Grandpa came in and sat down next to us. He ran his wrinkled fingers through his thinning gray hair.

"Better," Clark answered, pushing his glasses up his nose.

"Pet her?" Grandpa hollered. "Sure! If you think that will help."

After dinner, Mom, Dad, Grandma, and Grandpa talked and talked — about practically everything that had happened since they last saw each other. Nine years ago.

Clark and I were bored. Really bored.

"Can we, um, watch television?" Clark finally asked.

"Oh, sorry, dear," Grandma apologized. "We don't have a television."

Clark glowered at me — as if it was my fault.

"Why don't you call Arnold?" I suggested. Arnold is the biggest nerd in our neighborhood. And Clark's best friend. "Remind him to pick up your new comic."

"Okay," Clark grumbled. "Um, where's the phone?"

"In town." Grandma smiled weakly. "We don't know many people — still alive. Doesn't pay to have a phone. Mr. Donner — at the general store — he takes messages for us."

"Haven't seen Donner all week, though," Grandpa added. "Our car broke down. Should be fixed soon. Any day now."

No television.

No phone.

No car.

In the middle of a swamp.

This time it was my turn to glower — at Mom and Dad.

I put on my angriest face. I was sure they were going to take us to Atlanta with them now. Absolutely sure.

Dad glanced at Mom. He opened his mouth to speak. Then he turned toward me. And shrugged an apology.

"Guess it's time for bed!" Grandpa checked his watch. "You two have to get an early start," he said to Mom and Dad.

"Tomorrow you're going to have so much fun," Grandma assured Clark and me.

"Yes, indeed," Grandpa agreed. "This big old house is great to explore. You'll have a real adventure!"

"And I'm going to bake my famous rhubarb pie!" Grandma exclaimed. "You kids can help me. You'll love it. It's so sweet, your teeth will fall out after one bite!"

I heard Clark gulp.

I groaned — loudly.

Mom and Dad ignored us. They said good night. And good-bye. They were leaving real early in the morning. Probably before we got up.

We followed Grandma up the dark, creaky old steps and down a long, winding hall to our rooms on the second floor.

Clark's room was right next to mine. I didn't have a chance to see what it looked like. After Clark went in, Grandma quickly ushered me to my room.

My room. My gloomy room.

I set my suitcase down next to the bed and glanced around. The room was nearly as big as a gym! And it didn't have a single window.

The only light came from a dim yellow bulb in a small lamp next to the bed.

A handmade rug covered the floor. Worn thin in spots, its rings of color were dingy with age.

A warped wooden dresser sat against the wall opposite the bed. It leaned to one side. The drawers hung out.

A bed. A lamp. A dresser.

Only three pieces of furniture in this huge, windowless room.

Even the walls were bare. Not a single picture covered the dreary gray paint.

I sat down on the bed. I leaned against the bars of the iron headboard.

I ran my fingers over the blanket. Scratchy wool. Scratchy wool that smelled of mothballs.

"No way I'm going to use that blanket," I said out loud. "No way." But I knew I would. The room was cold and damp, and I began to shiver.

I quickly changed into my pajamas and pulled the smelly old blanket over me.

I twisted and turned. Trying to get comfortable on the lumpy mattress.

I stared up at the ceiling and listened. Listened to the night sounds of the creepy old house. Strange creaking noises that echoed through the old walls.

Then I heard the howls.

Frightening animal howls on the other side of the wall.

The sad howls from the swamp.

I sat up.

Were they coming from Clark's room?

6

I listened hard, afraid to move.

Another long, sad howl. From outside. Not from Clark's room.

"Stop it!" I scolded myself. "Clark is the one with the wild imagination. Not you!"

But I couldn't shut out the eerie howls from the swamp.

Was it an animal? Was it a swamp monster?

I pressed the pillows over my face. It took me hours to fall asleep.

When I woke up, I didn't know if it was morning — or the middle of the night. Without a window, it was impossible to tell.

I read my watch — 8:30. Morning.

I searched through the suitcase for my new pink T-shirt. I needed something to cheer me up — and pink is my favorite color. I pulled on my jeans. Slipped on my muddy sneakers.

I dressed quickly. The room reminded me of a prison cell. I wanted to escape fast.

I opened the bedroom door and peeked into the hall.

Empty.

But there, across from my room, I saw a small window. I hadn't noticed it the night before.

A bright ray of sunshine filtered through the dusty glass. I peered outside — into the swamp.

A heavy mist hung over the red cypress trees, casting a soft, rosy glow over the wet land. The glowing mist made the swamp look mysterious and unreal.

Something purple fluttered on a nearby tree limb. A purple bird. A purple bird with a bright orange beak. I'd never seen a bird like that before.

Then I heard the sounds again.

The horrible howls. The shrill cries.

From animals hiding deep in the swamp — all kinds of creatures I'd probably never seen before.

Swamp creatures.

Swamp monsters.

I shuddered. Then turned away from the window and headed for Clark's room.

I knocked on the door. "Clark!"

No answer.

"Clark?"

Silence.

I burst through the door and let out a cry.

About the Author

R.L. STINE is the author of the series *Fear Street*, *Nightmare Room*, *Give Yourself Goosebumps*, and the phenomenally successful *Goosebumps*. His thrilling teen titles have sold more than 250 million copies internationally — enough to earn him a spot in the *Guinness Book of World Records*! Mr. Stine lives in New York City with his wife, Jane, and his son, Matt.

YOU'VE READ THE BOOKS...
NOW OWN THE THRILLS ON DVD

BRING HOME THE EXCITEMENT!

**R.L. Stine Classics
Come To DVD
For The First Time
From Twentieth Century
Fox Home Entertainment!**

www.foxhome.com

SCHOLASTIC
www.scholastic.com/

Collect Them All!

Goosebumps®

By R.L. Stine

- ❏ Goosebumps: Abominable Snowman of Pasadena
- ❏ Goosebumps: Attack of the Jack-O-Lanterns
- ❏ Goosebumps: Attack of The Mutant
- ❏ Goosebumps: Bad Hare Day
- ❏ Goosebumps: Barking Ghost
- ❏ Goosebumps: The Beast from the East
- ❏ Goosebumps: Be Careful What You Wish For...
- ❏ Goosebumps: The Cuckoo Clock of Doom
- ❏ Goosebumps: The Curse of Camp Cold Lake
- ❏ Goosebumps: Curse of the Mummy's Tomb
- ❏ Goosebumps: Deep Trouble
- ❏ Goosebumps: Egg Monsters from Mars
- ❏ Goosebumps: Ghost Beach
- ❏ Goosebumps: Ghost Camp
- ❏ Goosebumps: Ghost Next Door
- ❏ Goosebumps: The Girl Who Cried Monster
- ❏ Goosebumps: Go Eat Worms!
- ❏ Goosebumps: The Haunted Mask
- ❏ Goosebumps: The Haunted Mask II
- ❏ Goosebumps: The Headless Ghost
- ❏ Goosebumps: The Horror at Camp Jellyjam
- ❏ Goosebumps: How I Got My Shrunken Head
- ❏ Goosebumps: How to Kill a Monster
- ❏ Goosebumps: It Came from Beneath the Sink!
- ❏ Goosebumps: Lets Get Invisible
- ❏ Goosebumps: Monster Blood
- ❏ Goosebumps: Monster Blood II
- ❏ Goosebumps: A Night in Terror Tower
- ❏ Goosebumps: Night of the Living Dummy
- ❏ Goosebumps: Night of the Living Dummy II
- ❏ Goosebumps: Night of the Living Dummy III
- ❏ Goosebumps: One Day at HorrorLand
- ❏ Goosebumps: Piano Lessons Can Be Murder
- ❏ Goosebumps: Revenge of the Lawn Gnomes
- ❏ Goosebumps: Say Cheese and Die!
- ❏ Goosebumps: Say Cheese and Die — Again!
- ❏ Goosebumps: The Scarecrow Walks at Midnight
- ❏ Goosebumps: Shocker on Shock Street
- ❏ Goosebumps: Stay Out of the Basement
- ❏ Goosebumps: Vampire Breath
- ❏ Goosebumps: Welcome to Camp Nightmare
- ❏ Goosebumps: Welcome to Dead House
- ❏ Goosebumps: The Werewolf of Fever Swamp
- ❏ Goosebumps: Why I'm Afraid of Bees
- ❏ Goosebumps: You Can't Scare Me!

■ SCHOLASTIC

Read at Your Own Risk
Goosebumps
By R. L. Stine

Goosebumps®

Would You Dare Visit a Place That Ghosts, Mummies, Vampires, and Other Creepy Creatures Call Home?

GHOULISH GAMES

BEASTLY BOOKS

SPOOKY STORIES

www.scholastic.com/ goosebumps/books

THE MONSTER MOB

ACTIVITIES

AUTHOR INFO

AND MORE!

Once you're there, you may never come back.